THE LOOKING-GLASS

MACHADO DE ASSIS

THE
LOOKING-GLASS

Essential Stories

Translated from the Portuguese
by Daniel Hahn

PUSHKIN PRESS
LONDON

Pushkin Press
65-69 Shelton Street
London WC2H 9HE

English translation © 2022 Daniel Hahn

'The Fortune-Teller' was first published as 'A Cartomante'
in *Gazeta de Notícias do Rio de Janeiro* in 1884

'The Posthumous Portrait Gallery' was first published
as 'Galeria Póstuma' in *Volume do contos*, 1884

'The Loan' was first published as 'O Empréstimo' in *Gazeta de Notícias*, 1881

'The Tale of the Cabriolet' was first published as 'Anedota
do Cabriolet' in *Almanaque Brasileiro Garnier* in 1905

'The Stick' was first published as 'O Caso da
Vara' in *Gazeta de Notícias*, 1891

'The Secret Cause' was first published as 'A Causa Secreta'
in *Gazeta de Notícias* in 1885

'The Canon, or Metaphysics of Style' was first published as 'O
Cônego ou Metafisica do Estilo' in *Gazeta de Notícias* in 1885

'The Alienist' was first published as 'O Alienista' in instalments
in *A Estação* between October 1881 and March 1882

'The Looking-Glass' was first published as 'O
Espelho' in *Gazeta de Notícias* in 1882

'Midnight Mass' was first published as 'Missa
do Galo' in *Gazeta de Notícias* in 1893

This translation first published by Pushkin Press in 2022

Frontispiece © The Picture Art Collection / Alamy Stock Photo

1 3 5 7 9 8 6 4 2

ISBN 13: 978-1-78227-807-8

Typeset by Hewer Text UK Ltd, Edinburgh

Printed and bound by TJ Books Ltd, Padstow,
Cornwall on Munken Premium White 80gsm

www.pushkinpress.com

THE LOOKING-GLASS

CONTENTS

THE FORTUNE-TELLER

HAMLET REMARKS TO Horatio that there are more things in heaven and earth than are dreamed of in our philosophy. This was the same explanation that the lovely Rita gave to the youth Camilo, one Friday in November 1869, when he was teasing her over her previous night's visit to a fortune-teller; she used different words, though.

"Go on, laugh away. You men are all alike; you don't believe in anything. But you should know that I went, and that she guessed the reason for my visit before I had even told her. She was only just starting to lay out the cards and she said, 'There is somebody that Miss likes . . .' I admitted that I did indeed like somebody, and then she went on laying out the cards, then she rearranged them, and finally she declared that I was afraid you would forget me, but that no such thing would happen . . ."

"She was mistaken!" Camilo interrupted her, laughing.

"Oh, do not say such things, Camilo. If you only knew the state I have been in lately, on your account. You do know; I have told you already. Do not laugh at me, do not . . ."

Camilo took her hands and stared at her, serious. He swore that he loved her very much, that her feelings of alarm were as a child's; in any case, he said, whenever she had any fears, he was himself the best fortune-teller she could find. Then he scolded her; he said it was reckless to go to such places. Vilela might learn of it, and then . . .

"What do you mean, learn of it! I took the greatest of care when entering the house."

"Where is this place?"

"Not far from here, on the Rua da Guarda Velha; there was nobody around when I went. You can rest easy, Camilo; I am not mad."

Camilo laughed again.

"You truly believe in such things?" he asked her.

It was then that she, not realising that she was translating Hamlet into the vernacular, told him that there were many things in this world that were mysterious and true. If he did not believe, no matter; but the fact was, the fortune-teller had divined everything. And what else? The proof was that she was now calm and contented.

I think he was about to speak, but he held back. He did not want to snatch away her illusions. He, too, as a child, and even for some time afterwards, had been superstitious, he had held an entire arsenal of beliefs, which his mother had instilled in him and which disappeared when he was twenty. On the day when he let all that parasitic vegetation fall away, leaving nothing but the trunk of religion, he, having learned both teachings from his mother, enveloped both in the same doubt, then straight away in one single total denial. Camilo did not believe in anything. Why? He could not say, he possessed not one single argument: he merely denied everything. But I misspeak, because to deny is still to make a statement, and he never formulated his unbelief into words; faced with mystery, he contented himself with a shrug, and walked on.

They parted happy, he more so than she. Rita was sure that she was loved; Camilo not only had that certainty, but he had also seen her tremble and take risks for him, resorting to fortune-tellers, and however much he scolded her, he could not help but feel flattered. The site of their encounter was a house on the old Rua dos Barbonos, home to a woman from Rita's province. Rita walked down the Rua das Mangueiras, towards Botafogo, where she lived; Camilo went down

Guarda Velha, giving the fortune-teller's house a pass-ing glance.

Vilela, Camilo and Rita, three names, one love affair and no explanation of origins. So let us do that. The first two were childhood friends. Vilela went into the magistracy. Camilo joined the civil service, against the wishes of his father who had hoped to see him a doctor; but his father died, and Camilo preferred to be nothing at all, until his mother procured a government job for him. At the start of 1869, Vilela returned from the provinces, where he had married a beautiful and silly woman; he quit the magistracy and came here to open a lawyer's office. Camilo procured a house for him over by Botafogo, and he boarded ship to receive him.

"Is it really you, senhor?" exclaimed Rita, holding out her hand. "You cannot imagine how highly my husband esteems you, he never stops speaking of you."

Camilo and Vilela exchanged a tender look. Truly, they were friends.

Later, Camilo admitted to himself that Vilela's wife did not belie her husband's letters. It was indeed so, she was charming and lively in gesture, her eyes warm, her mouth delicate and questioning. She was a little older than the two of them: she had turned thirty, Vilela twenty-nine and Camilo twenty-six. However,

Vilela's serious bearing made him seem older than his wife, while Camilo was a naïve man in moral and practical experience alike. He lacked both the effects of time and those crystal spectacles that nature puts on some people's cradles to hasten their years. Neither experience, nor intuition.

The three of them formed a close bond. Familiarity brought intimacy. Not long afterwards, Camilo's mother died, and in this calamity, for such it truly was, the couple proved great friends to him. Vilela took care of the burial, the service and the probate arrangements; Rita dealt especially with his heart, and no one could have done it better.

How they proceeded from there to love, he would never know. The truth is, he enjoyed spending his hours by her side; she was his spiritual nurse, almost a sister, but most of all she was a woman and beautiful. *Odor di feminina*: that is what he inhaled from her, and around her, incorporating it into himself. They read the same books, they went to the theatre and took walks together. Camilo taught her draughts and chess and they would play in the evenings – she badly – he, as a kindness to her, only slightly less so. Thus it was, so far as things are concerned. But now comes the person herself, Rita with her wilful eyes, which often sought out his, consulted his before they did her husband's, with her cold hands, her unusual attitudes. One day, his birthday, he received from Vilela the gift of a fine walking-stick and from Rita only a card with a common greeting in pencil, and it was then that he was able to read within his own heart; he could not take his eyes off the little note. Just a few common words; and yet common things can sometimes be sublime, or, at the very least, delightful. The old calèche for hire, in which you first took a ride with your beloved, the two of you shut cosily away, is worth no less than Apollo's chariot. Thus man is; thus are the things that surround him.

Camilo sincerely wanted to escape, but he no longer could. Rita, like a serpent, was closing in, enfolding him entirely, making his bones spasm and crack, and dripping venom into his mouth. He was dazed and overpowered. Shame, fears, remorse, desires, every feeling seemed mixed together, but the battle was a short one and the victory thrilling. Farewell, scruples! It was not long before the shoe was fitting comfortably onto the foot, and off they both went, up the road, arm in arm, treading carelessly over grasses and gravel, suffering nothing more than a faint pang of heartache whenever they were apart. Vilela's trust and affection continued unchanged. One day, however, Camilo received an anonymous letter, which called him immoral and treacherous, and declared that the affair was known to all. Camilo was afraid, and, to deflect any suspicions, he took to visiting Vilela's house less and less often. His friend noticed his absences. Camilo replied that the cause was some frivolous boyish passion. Innocence bred cunning. The absences stretched out further, then the visits ceased entirely. It could be that a little self-regard also came into this, an intention to diminish the husband's kindnesses, so as to soften the betrayal in the act.

It was around this time that Rita, suspicious and fearful, visited the fortune-teller to consult her as to the true cause of Camilo's behaviour. As we have seen, the fortune-teller did restore her trust, and the young man scolded her for having done what she did. A few more weeks went by. Camilo received another two or three letters, so impassioned a warning that they could not originate purely from virtue, but rather from the spite of some rival; this was Rita's opinion, who, though using less well-shaped words, formulated this thought: virtue is lazy and mean, it does not expend time or paper; only self-interest is active and lavish.

Not that Camilo was any more reassured by this; he was fearful lest the anonymous person go to Vilela, at which point the disaster would become irredeemable. Rita agreed that this was a possibility.

"Well," she said, "I will take the addressed envelopes to compare their handwriting with the letters that arrive at home; if any of them are the same, I will remove them and tear them up . . ."

None came; but a while later Vilela started to appear grim, speaking little, as if distrustful. Rita hurried to tell the other man this, and they pondered it. Her opinion was that Camilo ought to return to their house, to sound her husband out, possibly learning from him of some private business concern. Camilo disagreed; to show up now after so many months' absence would be to confirm a suspicion or accusation. Better that they take great care, making the sacrifice for a few weeks. They agreed upon their means of communication, in case of necessity, and parted with tears.

The following day, while at work, Camilo received this note from Vilela: "Come now, right now, to our house; I must speak to you without delay." It was gone noon. Camilo left at once; on the street, he realised that it would have been more natural to summon him to his office; why home? Everything suggested that this was an uncommon matter, and the handwriting, whether reality or illusion, looked shaky to him. He combined all these things with the previous day's news.

"Come now, right now, to our house; I must speak to you without delay," he repeated to himself, his eyes on the piece of paper.

In his mind, he saw the emerging climax of a drama, Rita subdued and tearful, Vilela outraged, taking his nib and writing this note, certain that Camilo would present himself, and waiting there to kill him. Camilo shuddered, afraid: then he gave a half-hearted smile, for in any case the idea of refusing appalled him, and he walked on. On the way, he thought to go home; he might find some message from Rita, explaining everything. He found nothing, and no one. Back out on the street, he found the idea of their having been discovered more and more believable; an anonymous accusation was quite plausible, even from the same person who had threatened him previously; perhaps Vilela knew everything now. That suspension of his visits, for no apparent reason, on a trivial pretext, would only have confirmed the rest.

Camilo kept walking, anxious and on edge. Although he was not rereading the note, its words were memories, fixed right there before his eyes, or otherwise – which was even worse – they were murmured into his ear, in Vilela's own voice. "Come now, right now, to our house; I must speak to you without delay." Spoken like this, in the other man's voice, their tone was mysterious and threatening. Come now, right now, for what? It was nearly one in the afternoon. His distress was growing by the minute. No question but that he was afraid. It occurred to him that he might go armed, considering that, if there was nothing to it, there was no harm done, and the precaution could be useful. Then straight away he rejected the idea, annoyed at himself, and continued, picking up pace, towards the Largo da Carioca, in order to take a tilbury. He arrived, climbed in, and ordered the coachman to proceed at a canter.

"The sooner the better," he thought. "I cannot continue like this . . ."

But even the trotting of the horse seemed to worsen his distress. Time was flying, and he would not be long in facing the danger. Almost at the Rua da Guarda Velha, the tilbury had to stop, the street obstructed by an overturned cart. Deep down, Camilo was glad of the obstacle, and he waited. After five minutes, he noticed that beside him, on the left, exactly beside the tilbury, was the house of the fortune-teller whom Rita had once consulted, and he had never been so eager to believe in the lessons of cards. He looked over at the house and saw its windows closed, while all the rest were open and swarming with people curious about the incident on the road. One might think it the home of an indifferent Fate.

Camilo sat back in the tilbury, so as not to see anything. His agitation was great, extraordinary, and from the depths of his spiritual layers, ghosts from another time were emerging, his old beliefs, his early superstitions. The coachman suggested that they return to the first side street and take another route; he replied no, that they would wait. And he leaned forward to look at the house . . . Then he made a gesture of disbelief: it was the notion that he could hear the fortune-teller, an idea flapping past him, in the distance, on vast grey wings; it disappeared, reappeared, and faded away again in his brain; but soon it moved its wings once more, closer now, circling . . . On the street, the men were shouting, trying to free the cart:

"Do it! Now! Push! Go on, go on!"

Soon enough, the obstacle would be removed. Camilo shut his eyes, thought about other things; but the husband's voice was whispering the words from the letter into his ear: "Come now, right now . . ." And he beheld the twists of the drama and trembled. The house was looking at him. His legs wanted to get out of the cab and go inside. Camilo seemed to be standing before a long opaque veil . . . he thought for a moment about the inexplicability of so many things.

His mother's voice was repeating a host of extraordinary stories, and the same line from the Prince of Denmark echoed within him: "There are more things in Heaven and Earth than are dreamed of in your philosophy." What would he stand to lose, if . . .?

He found himself on the pavement, at the door; he instructed the coachman to wait, moved quickly down the hallway, and climbed the stairs. The light was dim, the steps were worn, the bannister sticky; but he saw nothing, felt nothing. He climbed and knocked. Nobody appeared; he considered going back down, but it was too late, curiosity lashed his blood, his temples throbbed; he knocked again, one, two, three blows. A woman appeared; it was the fortune-teller. Camilo said he had come to consult her; she led him inside. From there, they climbed to the attic, up a staircase even worse than the first and darker. At the top, there was a small parlour, poorly lit by one window, which overlooked the roof at the back. Old pieces of furniture, dark walls, an air of poverty, which increased rather than destroyed the place's prestige.

The fortune-teller had him sit at the table, and she sat opposite him, her back to the window, so that what little light there was from outside struck Camilo full in the face. She opened a drawer and pulled out a deck of long, creased cards. While she shuffled them, quickly, she watched him, not directly face-on, but from beneath her lids. She was a woman of forty, Italian, dark and thin, with large, sly, sharp eyes. She turned three cards over onto the table, and said:

"Let us see, first of all, what has brought you here, senhor. Ah, you are having quite a scare . . ."

Camilo, marvelling, nodded.

"And you want to know," she continued, "if something is going to happen to you or not . . ."

"To me and to her," he explained, animatedly.

The fortune-teller did not smile; she merely told him to wait. Quickly she picked up the cards again and shuffled them with her long thin fingers, their nails neglected; she shuffled them well, cut the decks, once, twice, thrice; then she began to spread them out. Camilo kept his eyes on her, curious and worried.

"The cards tell me . . ."

Camilo leaned forward to imbibe each one of her words. Then she declared that he had nothing to fear. Nothing would happen to him, nor to anybody else; he, the third party, knew nothing. This notwithstanding, a great deal of caution was essential: spites and envies were bubbling up around them. She talked to him about the love that bound them, about Rita's beauty . . . Camilo was amazed. The fortune-teller concluded her task, gathered the cards back up and shut them in the drawer.

"You have restored some peace to my soul, senhora," he said, reaching his hand across the table and squeezing the fortune-teller's.

She stood up, laughing.

"Go," she said, "go, *ragazzo innamorato . . .*"

And standing there before him, with her index finger, she touched his forehead. Camilo shuddered, as if hers were the hand of the sibyl herself, and he stood, too. The fortune-teller went to the bureau, on which there sat a dish of raisins; she took a bunch, began to pull them off the stalk and eat them, showing two rows of teeth that belied the neglect of her nails. Even in this commonplace action, there was something unusual about the woman. Camilo, though anxious to leave, was unsure how to pay; he did not know the price.

"Raisins cost money," he said at last, taking out his wallet. "How many would you like to send for?"

"Ask your heart," she replied.

Camilo removed a ten-mil-réis note, and handed it to her. The fortune-teller's eyes flashed. The usual price was two mil-réis.

"I can see you like her very much, senhor . . . And so you should; she likes you very much, too. Go, go, easy now. Take care on the staircase, it's dark; put on your hat . . ."

The fortune-teller had already put the banknote into her pocket, and she accompanied him down, talking, with a slight accent. Camilo said goodbye to her downstairs, and descended the lower staircase that took him to the street, while the fortune-teller, happy with her payment, went back up, humming a barcarole. Camilo found the tilbury waiting; the road was clear. He got in and they resumed their journey at a canter.

Everything seemed better to him now, things had a new aspect, the sky was limpid and the faces cheerful. He even laughed at his fears, calling them childish; he recalled the words in Vilela's letter and saw that they were friendly and familiar. Where had he seen any threat? He could tell, too, that they were urgent, and that he had been wrong to delay as he had; it could be the very gravest of matters.

"Go on, quickly, go on," he said again to the coachman.

And to himself, to explain his delay to his friend, he invented something; it seems he also formed a plan to take advantage of the incident to return to their previous regularity . . . And along with his plans, the words of the fortune-teller resounded in his soul. Truly she had divined the purpose of his consultation, his condition, the existence of a third party; why should she not have divined the rest? The present unknown is no different from the future. So it was, slow and persistent, that the young man's old beliefs were being restored to their supremacy, and mystery seized him with fingernails of iron. At times he wanted to laugh, and he did laugh at himself, somewhat vexed; but the woman, the cards, those clipped, positive words, then the exhortation: Go, go, *ragazzo innamorato*; and at the end, in the distance, that barcarole of farewell, slow and graceful, these were the recent elements which, together with the old ones, formed a faith that was lively and new.

The truth is, his heart was glad now and impatient, thinking of happy hours gone by and those yet to come. As the cab passed through Glória, Camilo looked out to sea, reaching his eyes far to where the water and the sky meet in an infinite embrace, and thus he had a sense of the future – a long, long, endless future.

Soon he arrived at Vilela's house. He stepped out, pushed the metal garden gate and entered. The house was silent. He climbed the six stone steps, and barely had time to knock before the door opened, and Vilela appeared.

"My apologies, I couldn't get here earlier; what is the matter?"

Vilela did not reply; his features were discomposed; he gestured to Camilo and they walked into a small inner room. As he stepped inside, Camilo could not contain a scream of horror: at the back of the room, on the sofa, Rita lay dead and bloody. Vilela took him by the collar, and with two shots from his revolver, laid him out dead on the floor.

THE POSTHUMOUS
PORTRAIT GALLERY

I

No, THERE IS simply no way to describe the dismay caused across the whole of Engenho Velho, and particularly in the hearts of his friends, by the death of Joaquim Fidélis. Nothing more unexpected. He was strong, in cast-iron health, and he had been to a dance on the very night before, where all those present saw him conversing and happy. He even danced himself, at the invitation of a woman in her sixties, the widow of a friend, who took him by the arm and said:

"Come along now, let's show these whippersnappers what we oldies can do."

Joaquim Fidélis protested, smiling; but he obeyed and he danced. It was two o'clock when he left, wrapping his sixty years in a thick cloak – we were in June 1879 at that time – putting his bald head into his hood, lighting a cigar, and stepping nimbly into his carriage.

In the carriage he might have dozed; but at home, despite the hour and the great weight of his eyelids, he still went to his desk, opened a drawer, took out one of several handwritten booklets – and spent three or four minutes writing ten or eleven lines. His last words were these: "In short, a frightful evening; some long-in-the-tooth reveller forced me to dance a quadrille with her; at the door this yokel asked me for a gift. Frightful!" He put the notebook away, undressed, got into bed, fell asleep and died.

Yes, the news dismayed the whole neighbour-hood. So loved was he, with those beautiful manners, able to talk to anybody, well-educated with those who were well-educated, ignorant with the ignorant, youthful with the youths, and even girlish with the girls. And then so obliging, ready to write letters, to talk to friends, to fix quarrels, to lend money. In his home he would gather some of his closest acquaint-ances from the neighbourhood, and sometimes from other areas, too; they would play ombre or whist, they would talk about politics. Joaquim Fidélis had been a member of the chamber of deputies until the chamber was dissolved by the Marquis of Olinda, in 1863. Failing to get re-elected, he quit public life. He was a conservative, though he accepted the label only with great difficulty, believing it a political Gallicism. One of the Saquarema group, that was what he liked to be called. But he relinquished everything; it seemed he had lately disconnected from his own party, and finally even from their views. There are reasons to believe that, from a certain point in time, he had been a profound sceptic, and nothing more.

He was rich and well-schooled. He had graduated in Law in 1842. Now he did nothing, and read a lot. He had no women in the house. A widower since the first wave of yellow fever, he refused any second marriage, to the great grief of three or four ladies, who had been nurturing that particular hope for some time. One of them even perfidiously prolonged her beautiful curls of 1845 until she was a grandmother twice over; another, a younger woman, likewise widowed, thought to keep him with some concessions as generous as they were irreparable. "My dear Leocádia," he would say on those occasions when she hinted at a matrimonial solution, "why do we not continue just as we are? Mystery is the very charm of life." He lived with a nephew, Benjamim, the son of a sister, orphaned from a tender age. Joaquim Fidélis raised him and got him into his studies, the boy eventually receiving a bachelor's diploma in the legal sciences, in the year 1877.

Benjamim was in a daze. He could not take in his uncle's death. He had run to the bedroom, found a corpse in the bed, cold, his eyes open, a slight ironic curl on the left corner of his mouth. He wept and wept. He had not lost any mere relative but a father, a tender and devoted father, a unique heart. Benjamim, at last, wiped away his tears; and because it pained him to see the dead man's eyes open, and especially the curled lip, he corrected both of those things. The dead man thus received his tragic expression; but the originality of the mask was lost.

"Don't say that!" one of the neighbours, Diogo Vilares, was soon shouting, when he learned of the event.

Diogo Vilares was one of Joaquim Fidélis's five principal intimates. He owed him the job that he had been doing since 1857. Now he came over to the house, followed by the other four, who arrived right after him, one by one, stunned, incredulous. First came Elias Xavier, who had attained through the intercession of the deceased, it was said, a commendation; then João Bras, a member of parliament who was, under the substitutes rule, elected with Joaquim Fidélis's influence. Then, finally, came Fragoso and Galdino, who did not owe him diplomas, commendations or jobs, but other favours. To Galdino he had advanced some small amount of capital, and for Frangoso he had arranged a good marriage . . . And now dead! Dead for ever! Standing around the bed of the deceased, they gazed at the serene face and recalled their final party, from last Sunday, so intimate, so jovial! And, closer still, two nights ago, when the usual rounds of ombre went on until eleven.

"Do not come tomorrow," Joaquim Fidélis had said to them. "I shall be at Carvalhinho's dance."

"And after that . . .?"

"The night after tomorrow, I will be here."

And as they left, he had even given them a packet of very fine cigars, as he did on occasion, with the addition of some sweets for the little ones, and two or three refined jokes . . . All faded away! All scattered! All over!

The burial was attended by many important people: two senators, an ex-minister, noblemen, men of means, lawyers, traders, doctors; but the coffin-handles were held by the five close friends and Benjamim. None of them wanted to yield this final favour to anybody else, considering it a personal and non-transferable duty. The valediction at the cemetery was spoken by João Brás, a touching farewell, with rather too much style for such a sudden event, but, still, excusable. Once the shovelful of earth had been thrown, every mourner moved away from the grave, apart from the six of them, who watched the gravediggers go about the rest of their indifferent work. They did not step away until they had seen the grave filled up, and the funeral wreaths placed atop it.

II

THE SEVENTH-DAY MASS gathered them all together again in the church. When the mass was over, the five friends accompanied the dead man's nephew back to the house. Benjamim invited them to join him for lunch.

"I hope Uncle Joaquim's friends will be my friends, too," he said.

They went in, they had lunch. At lunch they talked about the dead man; each of them told a little anecdote, shared a witticism; they were unanimous in their praise and their feelings of loss. After the meal, since they had asked for something to remember the deceased by, they moved into the study, and chose freely: one man an old pen, another a glasses case, a pamphlet, some private remnant or other. Benjamim felt consoled. He informed them that he intended to preserve the study just so. He had not even opened the desk. He did open it then, however, and, with them, inventoried the contents of some drawers. Letters, loose pieces of paper, concert programmes, menus from some superb dinners, everything jumbled and muddled together. Among other things, they found a few handwritten notebooks, numbered and dated.

"A journal!" said Benjamim.

It was, indeed, a journal with the deceased's impressions, like secretly kept memories, a man's confidences to himself. Great was the friends' emotion; to read it was to be talking to him still. Such an upright character! Such a discreet soul! Benjamim began to read, but his voice quickly choked up, and João Brás continued.

Their interest in the writing numbed the pain of the death. It was a book worthy of the printing-press. Much political and social observation, much philo-sophical reflection, some stories about public men, about Feijó, about Vasconcelos, other stories that were purely amorous, the names of ladies, Leocádia among them; a collection of events and comments. Each man marvelled at the deceased's skill, the charms of his style, the interest of his subject-matter. Some shared their opinions about typographical printing; Benjamim agreed, on the condition that certain things be excluded, their being either inappropriate or excessively private. And they continued to read, skipping over pieces and pages, until the clock struck noon. They all got up; Diogo Vilares was already going to arrive at the office out of hours; João Brás and Elias had somewhere to be together; Galdino was going on to the store; Fragoso needed to change out of his black garb to accompany his wife to the Rua do Ouvidor. They agreed to meet again to continue their reading. Certain details had given them an itching of scandal, and itches need to be scratched: which is what they hoped to do, by reading.

"Until tomorrow, then," they said.

"Until tomorrow."

Once alone, Benjamim continued to read what his uncle had written. Among other things, he did admire the portrait of the widow Leocádia, a masterpiece of patience and likeness, even if the date coincided with that of their affair. It was evidence of a rare impartiality of spirit. As for the others, the deceased was excellent in his portraits. Starting from 1873 or 1874, the notebooks were full of them, some of the living, others of the dead, a few of public men, Paula Sousa, Aureliano, Olinda, etc. They were brief and substantial, sometimes three or four bold strokes, of such fidelity and perfection that it was as if the figure had been photo-graphed. Benjamim kept reading; suddenly he came across Diogo Vilares. And he read these few lines:

DIOGO VILARES. – I have referred to this friend on many occasions, and I will do so on many more, if he does not first bore me to death, a skill in which I deem him a professional. He asked me years ago to secure some employment for him, which I did. He did not warn me in what currency he would be repaying me. What rare gratitude! He went so far as to compose a sonnet and publish it. He talked to me about the favour I had done him at every step, he paid me great compliments; at last, it stopped. Later we became more intimately acquainted. I came to know him even better then. *C'est le genre ennuyeux.* He is not a bad ombre partner. I am told he owes noth-ing to anybody. A good family man. Stupid and cred-ulous. In the space of four days, I have heard him say of one minister that he was excellent and loathsome – his interlocutors being different. He laughs a great deal and not well. Everybody, on their first encounter with him, supposes him a serious fellow; on the second day they click their fingers at him. The reason for this is his appearance, or more specifically, his cheeks, which lend him a rather superior air.

Benjamim's first sensation was of having escaped some danger. What if Diogo Vilares had been there? He reread the portrait and could barely believe his eyes; but there was no denying it, it was Vilares's own name, it was his uncle's own hand. And he was not the only one of the friends; Benjamim leafed through the pages and found Elias:

ELIAS XAVIER. – This Elias is a subordinate spirit, destined to serve, and to serve haughtily, like coachmen in an elegant house. He commonly treats my private visits with a certain arrogance and disdain: the politics of an ambitious flunky. From the first weeks, I understood that he wanted to make himself my closest friend; and I understood equally that, on the day he actually found himself in such a position, he would turf all the rest out onto the street. There are moments when he calls me into a window recess to talk in secret of the sun and the rain, his obvious purpose being to instil a suspicion in other people that there are private matters between us, which he does indeed achieve, because everybody is exceedingly courteous towards him. He is intelligent, cheerful and polite. He talks very well. I do not know any man quicker to understand. He is no coward, nor a slanderer. He only speaks ill of people out of self-interest; lacking any interest, he keeps quiet; true slander is gratuitous. Devoted and ingratiating. He has no ideas, this is true; but there is this one big difference between him and Diogo Vilares: Diogo repeats quickly and ignorantly those ideas that he hears, whereas Elias knows how to make them his own and plant them in the conversation at an opportune moment. One incident in 1865 is a good demonstration of the man's cunning. Having supplied a few freed slaves for the Paraguayan war, he was set to receive a commendation. He did not need me; but he came to ask me to intercede, two or three times, with a look of distress and much beseeching. I spoke to the minister, who replied: "Elias already knows that the order has been drawn up; all that is needed now is the Emperor's signature." I understood then that this was merely a strategy in order that he might acknowledge this obligation to me. A good ombre partner; a bit quarrelsome, but shrewd.

"Oh my, Uncle Joaquim!" exclaimed Benjamim, getting to his feet. And then, after a few moments, he mused: "I am reading a heart, an unpublished book. I knew the public edition, the revised and expurgated one. This is the primitive interior text, the precise and authentic text. But who ever would have imagined it . . . Oh my, Uncle Joaquim!"

And sitting back down, he re-read the portrait of Elias, at a leisurely pace, considering the characteristics. Although he lacked sufficient observation to allow him to evaluate the truth of what was written, he found it in many parts, at least, a good likeness. He compared these iconographical notes, so stark, so blunt, with his uncle's civil and charming manners, and felt himself overtaken by a certain terror and unease. And of himself, for example, what might the deceased have said of him? With this in mind, he leafed further through the pages, overlooking a few ladies, public men, found Fragoso – the briefest of sketches – and Galdino right after him, and João Brás four pages later. The first had just taken away a pen of his uncle's, maybe the very same with which the deceased had produced his portrait. The sketch was brief, and read thus:

FRAGOSO. – Honest, with sugary manners and handsome. It was no trouble to marry him off; he and his wife live very well together. I know he adores me extraordinarily – almost as much as he does himself. His talk is banal, polished and hollow.

GALDINO MADEIRA. – The best heart in the world

and a character without blemish; but the qualities of his mind destroy the others. I lent him some money, for family reasons, and because I did not need it. He has a kind of hole in his brain, through which his mind drains and falls into the void. He will never reflect for three minutes straight. He lives mostly on images, on borrowed phrases. The "teeth of calumny" and other expressions, as battered as old guest-house mattresses, are his delights. He is easily shamed at cards, and once shamed he makes a point of losing, and of showing that it is deliberate. He does not dismiss his bad shop assistants. If he did not have a bookkeeper, it is doubtful whether he could add up his own loose change. One subdelegate, a friend of mine who owed him a little money for two years, used to tell me with great mirth that whenever Galdino saw him on the street, instead of asking him to settle his debt, he would ask instead for news from the ministry.

João Brás. – No fool, and no dullard. Very attentive, albeit unmannerly. He cannot watch a minister's car driving past but he pales and looks away. I believe he is ambitious; but at his age, with no career, his ambition is turning gradually to envy. For the two years in which he served as a parliamentarian he fulfilled his role honourably: he worked hard, and made some good speeches, not brilliant ones, but solid, full of facts and thoughtful. The proof that he has retained a trace of ambition is the ardour with which he pursues certain prestigious or honorary posts; a few months ago, he agreed to be president of a São José brotherhood, and I am told that he fulfils that role with exemplary zeal. I do believe he is an atheist, but I cannot assert so much. He laughs little and discreetly. His life is pure and austere, but his character does have one or two fraudulent notes, which lack the artist's hand; on very small matters, he lies easily.

Benjamim, dumbstruck, found himself at last. "This nephew of mine," read the manuscript, "is twenty-four years old, he has a project for judicial reform, and a good head of hair, and he loves me. And I love him no less. Discreet, loyal, and good – good even to credulity. As steadfast in his affections as he is flexible in his opinions. Superficial, a friend to novelties, a lover in the Law of terminology and formulas."

He wanted to reread it, yet could not; those few lines felt like a mirror. He got up, walked over to the window, looked out at the estate and turned back inside to contemplate his features once again. He did contemplate them; they were few, sparse, but did not seem defamatory. If there had been an audience present, it is likely that the youth's feeling of mortification would have been lessened, because the need to dispel those other people's impression would have given him the necessary strength to react against what was written; but alone, by himself, he was obliged to tolerate it without contrast. Then he considered whether his uncle might not have composed these pages while in a bad mood; he compared them to others where the wording was less harsh, but he could not say whether the mildness there was deliberate or otherwise.

To confirm the theory, he recalled the deceased's usual manner, the times he spent in private, and in laughter, alone with him, or in talk with his other friends. He summoned up his uncle's picture, with that spirited and mild look in his eye, and his rather serious way of joking; in his place, instead of this frank and pleasant man, the image that appeared was of his uncle lying dead in his bed, eyes open, lip curled. He shook it from his mind, but the image remained. Unable to banish it, Benjamim tried mentally to shut the eyes and re-arrange the mouth; but just as soon as he did so, the eyelids rose again, and that irony curled his cheek. He was no longer the man, he was the author of the manuscript.

Benjamim dined badly and slept badly. The following day, in the afternoon, the five friends re-appeared to listen to the reading. They arrived anxious, eager; they asked him many questions; they were insistent in their requests to see the manuscript. But Benjamim prevaricated, he said one thing and then another, he made up pretexts; to his misfortune, he was visited in the living-room, behind the five men, by the eternal mouth of the deceased, and this circumstance made him more reticent still. He eventually turned cold, wishing to be left alone, in the hope that the vision might disappear with them. They spent thirty or forty minutes like this. Finally, the five men exchanged a look, and resolved to leave; they said their goodbyes formally, and left, still in conversation, for their homes.

"Ah, so different from his uncle! Such a chasm between them! The inheritance has quite puffed him up! Well, leave him be! Oh! Joaquim Fidélis! Oh! Joaquim Fidélis!"

THE LOAN

I SHALL SHARE AN anecdote, but an anecdote in the proper sense of the word, which has been commonly expanded to include short stories of pure invention. This one is true; I could cite several people who know it as well as I. Nor has it been hidden, but rather lacked a tranquil soul who might have found the philosophy within it. As you surely know, there is a philosophical meaning to all things. Carlyle discovered that of waistcoats, or, more precisely, of clothing; and nobody can be unaware that numbers, long before the Ipiranga lottery, comprised Pythagoras's theorem. For my part, I believe that I have deciphered this story of a loan; you will judge for yourself whether I am mistaken.

And we shall begin by amending Seneca. Each day, in the opinion of that moralist, is, in itself, a singular life; in other words, a life within life. I do not dispute this; but why did he not add that sometimes one single hour can be the representation of a life in its entirety? Behold this youth: he comes into the world with a great ambition, a ministerial portfolio, a bank, a viscount's coronet, a bishop's crozier. At fifty we will find him a humble customs-office drudge, or a country sacristan. Everything that occurred in thirty years, some Balzac or other could put into three hundred pages; why then might not life, which was Balzac's teacher, squeeze it into thirty or sixty minutes?

The clock had struck four at the registry office of the notary public Vaz Nunes, on Rua do Rosário. The clerks had just completed the final strokes of their pens; then they cleaned the goose quills on the corner of black silk that hung from the drawer beside them; they shut the drawers, tidied their papers, arranged their documents and their ledgers, washed their hands; some, who had changed coats at the door, now took off their work ones and pulled on their outdoor ones. Vaz Nunes was left alone.

This honest notary was one of the century's shrewdest men. He is dead: we now can praise him all we like. He had a lancet eye, cutting, sharp. He could guess the character of those who sought him out to draw up agreements or resolutions; he knew the soul of a testator long before the will had been concluded; he sniffed out secret tricks and hidden thoughts. He wore spectacles, just as notaries public do on the stage; but not being short-sighted, he peered over them, when he wished to see, and through them, when he meant not to be seen. Nobody slyer, said the clerks. In any case, a circumspect man. He was fifty, a widower, childless, and to speak like some of his fellow notaries, he was just nibbling his way through his two-hundred-conto assets, quietly.

"Who's there?" he asked suddenly, turning towards the door to the street.

At the door, standing on the step, was a man he did not immediately recognise, and even after a few moments still struggled to place. Vaz Nunes asked him please kindly to come in; the man obeyed, greeted him, held out his hand, then sat down beside the desk. He did not carry himself with the natural discomfort of a beggar; on the contrary, he gave the impression of having come only to bestow upon the notary something exceptionally precious and rare. And yet, Vaz Nunez gave a shudder, and waited.

"You don't remember me?"

"I don't . . ."

"We met one night, a few months back, in Tijuca . . . You do not recall? At Teodorico's house, that big Christmas Eve dinner; indeed, I toasted your health . . . Do you not remember Custódio?"

"Oh!"

Custódio, who had previously been somewhat hunched, now straightened up. He was a man of forty. He dressed poorly, but his hair was neatly brushed, he was tidy, correct. He wore his nails long, tended with great care, and his hands were very well shaped, and soft, unlike the skin on his face, which was rough. Trivial details; yet necessary, to complement a certain double aspect that distinguished this man, an aspect of both beggar and general. Walking on the street, penniless and lunchless, he nonetheless seemed to be leading an army behind him. The reason was no other than the contrast between his nature and his circumstances, between soul and life. This Custódio had been born with a vocation for wealth, but with no vocation for work. He had an instinct for elegance, a love of excess, of good food, of beautiful ladies, of fine carpets, of precious furniture, a voluptuary and, to some degree, an artist, capable of managing the Vila Torlonia or the gallery at the Hamilton Palace. But he had no money; neither money nor any aptitude or inclination for earning it; and yet he did need to live. *Il faut bien que je vive*, one claimant used to say to Minister Talleyrand. *Je n'en vois pas la nécessité*, the minister had retorted coolly. Nobody ever gave Custódio this answer; they would give him money, ten mil-réis from one, five from another, twenty from the next, and it was mainly from such disbursements as these that he paid for his lodging and his food.

I say he lived on them mainly, for Custódio did not object to involving himself occasionally in business, on the condition that he choose which business, and he always chose those that were entirely without worth. He had an excellent nose for calamities. Of twenty companies, he immediately guessed which one was the purest folly, and applied himself to that, with great determination. Ill-fortune, which pursued him, made the nineteen prosper, while the twentieth blew up in his hands. No matter: he would ready himself for the next.

On this occasion, for example, he had seen an advertisement from somebody seeking a partner, with a sum of five contos, to go into business, with the promise of eighty to a hundred contos of profit in the first six months. Custódio went to meet the advertiser. It was a great idea, a needle factory, a new industry with a tremendously promising future. And the plans, the designs for the factory, the reports from Birmingham, the import charts, the responses from the tailors, from the haberdashers, etc., every document from a lengthy process of inquiry passed before Custódio's eyes, which were starry with numbers he did not understand, numbers which for that very reason seemed indisputable. Twenty-four hours; he asked no more than twenty-four hours to deliver the five contos. And he left feeling flattered, encouraged by the advertiser who, still standing at the door, drowned him in a torrent of bank balances. But the five contos, less docile or less wayward than a mere five mil-réis might have been, shook their heads incredulously, and stayed put in their chests, impeded by fear and drowsiness. Nothing. Eight or ten friends to whom he spoke said they did not at present have the sum he requested, and nor did they believe in the factory. He had lost all hope when he happened to walk up Rua do Rosário and read the name Vaz Nunes on a registry-office door. He felt a shiver of happiness; he recalled Tijuca, the notary's manner, the words with which he had responded to the toast, and he told himself that this man was the saviour of the situation.

"I have come to ask you for a deed . . ."

Vaz Nunes, armed for a different opening, did not reply; he peered over his glasses and waited.

"A deed of gratitude," explained Custódio. "I have come to ask you a big favour, an essential favour, and I trust that my friend . . ."

"If it is within my gift . . ."

"The business is, please mark my words, an excellent one; a quite superb one. And I would never presume to trouble others with it, were I not certain of the outcome. The matter is all in hand; orders have already been sent to England; most likely, everything will be in place within two months, it is a brand-new industry. There are three of us in partnership, my share is five contos. I have come to ask you for this sum, for a six-month term – or three, at moderate interest . . ."

"Five contos?"

"Yes, senhor."

"But Senhor Custódio, I do not have a sum of that kind. Business is not good; and even if it were going well, I still could not spare so much. Who would ever expect five contos from a simple notary public?"

"Ah, but if you wanted to, senhor . . ."

"Oh, I do, no question; as I say, if it were a small amount, better fitted to my means, I would have no hesitation but to advance it to you. But five contos! Please believe me, it is quite impossible."

Custódio's soul fell flat. He had climbed Jacob's ladder up to heaven; but instead of descending like the angels in the biblical dream, he had rolled right back down and fallen flat. This was his last hope; and it was precisely because it was unhoped for that he had supposed it certain, since, like all hearts that surrender to the regime of whatsoever-may-come, Custódio's was superstitious. The poor devil felt his body being pricked with the millions of needles that the factory was forecast to produce in its first half-year. Unspeaking, his eyes still fixed on the ground, he hoped that the notary might continue, that he might feel some pity, might give him a chance; but the notary, who could read this in Custódio's soul, stayed silent too, turning his snuff-box between his fingers, taking deep breaths, with a rather insistent, nasal wheezing. Custódio rehearsed every attitude; now beggar, now general. The notary did not move. Custódio stood up.

"Well," he said, with just a flicker of spite, "then you must forgive me for troubling you . . ."

"Nothing to forgive; it is I who must apologise that I cannot be of service to you as I might have hoped. As I say: had the sum been less substantial, there would have been no question; but . . ."

He held his hand out to Custódio, who with his left had mechanically picked up his hat. The dull look in Custódio's eyes expressed the absorption of his soul, barely recovered from the fall that had consumed all his remaining energies. No mysterious ladder, no heaven; everything had flown away at a click of the notary's fingers. Farewell, needles! Reality returned, clasping him to it with nails of bronze. He would have to return to precarity, to accident, to the old bank account with its wide-eyed zeroes, and their currency symbols twisted ear-like, which would continue to stare at him and listen to him, to listen and to stare, prolonging the implacable digits of hunger. What a fall! And what an abyss! Facing reality at last, he looked at the notary with a gesture of farewell; but then a sudden idea illuminated the night-time of his brain. If the sum were smaller, Vaz Nunes could be of service to him, and he would do so with pleasure; why, then, might the sum not be smaller? He had even now given up the company; but he could not do the same with certain overdue rental payments, with two or three of his creditors, etc., and any reasonable sum, five hundred mil-réis, say, since the notary was inclined to lend it, would be most welcome. Custódio's soul perked up; he would live for the present, he had no interest at all in the past, or nostalgia, or fears, or regrets. The present was all. The present was the five hundred mil-réis, which he would soon behold rising from the notary's pocket, like a charter of liberty.

"Well," he said, "see what you can give me, and I will call upon other friends . . . How much?"

"I cannot say; but in truth, it would be only something very modest."

"Five hundred mil-réis?"

"No, I cannot do that."

"Not even five hundred mil-réis?"

"Not even that," the notary replied firmly. "Why are you surprised? I cannot deny, I do possess some properties; but please understand, my friend, I do not carry them around in my pocket; and I have private obligations of my own . . . Tell me, do you not have a job?"

"No, senhor."

"Look; I will give you something better than five hundred mil-réis; I will speak to the minister of justice, he and I are on good terms, and . . ."

Custódio interrupted him, slapping his palm down on his knee. Whether this was a natural movement, or a cunning diversion to avoid talking about the job, I cannot say; nor does it seem to matter much to the story. What does matter is that he persisted in his entreaty. So he could not give five hundred mil-réis? He would accept two hundred; two hundred would be enough, not for the company, since he was taking his friends' advice: he would turn it down. The two hundred mil-réis, seeing as the notary was willing to help him, was for an urgent necessity, "to plug a hole". And then he told him everything, answering candour with candour: that was the rule he lived by. He admitted that, when planning his dealings with that major

51

enterprise, he had considered also going to a persistent creditor, a devil, a Jew, who strictly speaking still owed him money, but who had treacherously double-crossed him. That was two hundred and something mil-réis; and ten, apparently; but he would accept two hundred . . .

"Truly, senhor, it grieves me to repeat what I have already told you; but, well, even those two hundred mil-réis I simply cannot give you. Even a hundred, if you asked for that, senhor, would be beyond my means on this occasion. On some other perhaps, and then no question, but now . . ."

"You cannot imagine the trouble I am in!"

"I repeat: not even a hundred. I have suffered many difficulties of late. Societies, subscriptions, masonry . . . Hard to believe, is it not? Naturally: a property-owner. My friend, it is very good to have houses – but you are not considering the damages, the repairs, the plumbing, the tithes, the insurance, the bad debts, etc. They are the holes in the pitcher, where most of the water ends up going . . ."

"Ah, if I only had a pitcher!" sighed Custódio.

"I do not disagree. What I am saying is that having houses does not prevent one's having concerns, expenses, and even creditors . . . Believe me, senhor, I have creditors of my own."

"Not even a hundred mil-réis!"

"Not even a hundred mil-réis, it grieves me to say it, but that is the truth. Not even a hundred mil-réis. What is the time?"

He stood up, and walked over to the middle of the room. Custódio followed, crawling, despairing. He could not quite believe that the notary public did not have at least a hundred mil-réis to hand. Who does not have a hundred mil-réis? He considered a pathetic scene, but the registry opened right onto the street; it would be ludicrous. He looked out. In the store opposite, a fellow was appraising a frock coat, standing at the doorway, because night was gathering and it was dark inside. The assistant was holding up the item; the customer was examining its cloth with his eyes and his fingers, followed by the stitches, the lining . . . This incident opened up a new horizon for him, albeit a modest one; it was time to retire the coat he was wearing. But the notary could not even give him fifty mil-réis. Custódio smiled – not out of scorn, not out of rage, but out of bitterness and doubt; surely it was impossible that he did not have fifty mil-réis. Twenty, at least? Not even twenty. Not twenty? No – it was all untrue, all lies. Custódio took out his handkerchief, smoothed his hat slowly; then he replaced the handkerchief, and straightened his necktie, with an expression of hope mixed with spite. He had been clipping the wings of his ambition, feather by feather; yet there remained a short fine down, which still gave him a fancy to fly. But from the other man, nothing at all. Vaz Nunes was checking the wall clock against his pocket-watch, he brought the latter up to his ear, cleaned the face, without a word, perspiring impatience and boredom through every pore. They were crawling towards five, and the notary public, who had been waiting for this, initiated his farewell. It was late; he lived far away. Saying this, he took off his alpaca coat and donned his cashmere one, moved the snuff-box from one to the other, and his handkerchief, and his wallet . . . Oh! His wallet! Custódio beheld this problematic implement, felt it up with his eyes; he envied the alpaca, he envied the cashmere, he wanted to be the pocket, he wanted to be the leather, the very material of that precious receptacle. And there it went; sunk deep into the inside-left breast pocket; the notary buttoned himself up. Not even twenty mil-réis! It was not possible that he hadn't twenty mil-réis in there, he thought; he would not say two hundred, but twenty, even if it could just be ten . . ."

"Right, then!" said Vaz Nunes, his hat on his head.

This was the fateful moment. Not a word from the notary, not even an invitation to dine with him; nothing; everything had come to an end. But great moments demand the greatest energy. Custódio felt all the force of this commonplace, and suddenly, quick as a shot, he asked the notary if he could not give him at least ten mil-réis.

"Would you like to look?"

And the notary unbuttoned his overcoat, took out his wallet, opened it, and showed him the two notes of five mil-réis.

"This is all I have," he said. "What I can do is share them with you, senhor; I shall give you one, and the other remains with me; would you find that satisfactory?"

Custódio accepted the five mil-réis, not sadly, nor grudgingly, but smiling, exhilarated, as if he had just conquered Asia Minor. Dinner was taken care of. He held his hand out to the other man, thanked him for the kindness, said goodbye until next time – a *see you again soon* that was full of implications. Then he left; the beggar faded at the registry door; it was the general who walked away, with a firm step and a fraternal nod to the English traders who were headed up the road towards the suburbs. Never had the sky seemed so blue, nor the evening so clear; the retinas of all men

THE TALE OF
THE CABRIOLET

"CABRIOLET'S HERE," SAID the slave who had come to the mother church of São José to fetch the priest, in order that he might administer last rites to two dying people.

Today's generation have seen nothing like the arrival and departure of the cabriolet in Rio de Janeiro. Nor would they know of the days when the cab and the tilbury occupied the role of our public or private vehicles. The cab did not last long. The tilbury, the earlier of the two, looks set to keep on going until the city has crumbled to dust. When it is all over and the diggers arrive, they will find a single one standing idle among the ruins, with the horse and coachman, now bones, awaiting their usual customers. They will be just as patient as today, however hard it rains, and their melancholy all the greater if the sun shines, for it will combine their current melancholy with that of the spectre of time past. The archaeologist will say curious things about the three skeletons. But the cabriolet had no history; it left only the tale I am about to tell.

"Two!" exclaimed the sacristan.

"Yes, senhor, two, Miss Anunciada and Master Pedrinho. Ah, poor Master Pedrinho! And oh, Miss Anunciada, the poor thing!" the slave wailed, pacing up and down, in distress, beside himself.

Any reader who finds his soul clouded by doubts, might naturally wonder whether the slave's feelings were genuine, or whether he merely wanted to arouse the interest of the curate and the sacristan. I believe that everything can be reconciled in this world, as in the next. I believe that he truly felt; yet nor do I disbelieve that he dearly longed to share some dreadful story. In any case, neither curate nor sacristan asked him a thing.

Not that the sacristan was not curious. Truthfully, he was rather more than that. He knew his parish by heart; he knew the names of the worshippers, knew of their lives, those of their husbands and their parents, each one's gifts and resources, and what they ate, what they drank, what they said, their garments and their goodness, the dowries of the unmarried ones, the behaviour of the married ones, the griefs of the widows. He researched everything: in between, he assisted at mass and all the rest. His name was João das Mercês, a man in his forties, with a thin grey beard, slim and of middling height.

"Which Pedrinho and Anunciada could they be?" he asked himself, as he followed the curate out.

Although he longed to know, the presence of the curate would hinder any questioning. The other man was so unspeaking and pious, walking towards the church door, that the sacristan was compelled to show the same silence and piety as he. Thus they went. The cabriolet was waiting for them; the coachman doffed his cap, the neighbours and a few passers-by kneeled, while priest and sacristan climbed inside and the vehicle slipped onto the Rua da Misericórdia. The slave hurriedly doubled back on his route, on foot.

There are donkeys and people walking the streets, and there are clouds in the sky, if the sky does have clouds, and there are thoughts in heads, if those heads do have thoughts. The sacristan's was filled with many that were various and muddled. Not about Our Father, though he knew how to adore him, nor about the holy water and the hyssop that he was carrying; and nor were they about the time – eight-fifteen at night – and as a matter of fact, the sky was clear and the moon was starting to show itself. Even the cabriolet, which was a new arrival, and which in this case was replacing the brougham, even this same vehicle did not occupy all of João das Mercês's brain, except insofar as it related to Master Pedrinho and Miss Anunciada.

"Must be new people," the sacristan was thinking, "but guests in somebody's home, no doubt, because there are no empty properties on the beachfront, and the number is Comendador Brito's house. Relatives, perhaps? But surely not relatives, for I never heard of them . . . Friends, no, not sure about that; maybe acquaintances, simple acquaintances. But then, would they send a cabriolet? This slave is new to the house himself; he must belong to one of the people dying, or to both."

Thus thought João das Mercês, but his thinking did not last long. The cabriolet stopped at the door of a house, which was indeed the home of Comendador Brito, José Martins de Brito. There were already a few people outside with candles; the priest and the sacristan got out and climbed the stairs, accompanied by the comendador. His wife, on the landing, kissed the priest's ring. Adults, children, slaves, a muffled murmur, dimly lit, and the two dying people waiting, each of them in their bedroom, at the back.

Everything happened as is customary and by the book on such occasions. Master Pedrinho was absolved and anointed, Miss Anunciada too, and the curate bade the house adieu to return to the mother church with the sacristan. The latter did not take his leave of the comendador without first asking quietly whether the two were relatives of his. No, not relatives, Brito replied; they were friends of a nephew who lived in Campinas; a terrible story . . . João das Mercês's eyes listened wide to those two words, and said, without speaking, that they would return to hear the rest – possibly that same night. It was all very quick, for the priest was on his way down the stairs, and he was compelled to go with him.

The fashion for cabriolets was so brief that this one probably never took another priest to minister to the dying. All that remained of it was an anecdote, which I will shortly be concluding, so slight was it, nothing to it at all. No matter. Whatever its size or importance, it was another slice of life for the sacristan, who helped the priest to store away the holy bread, to remove his surplice, and to do everything else, before saying good-bye and leaving. He left, at last, on foot, making his way up the beachfront road, until he came to a stop outside the comendador's house.

Along the way he had been summoning up that man's life, before and after he received the title. He assembled his business, which I believe was as a provi-sioner of ships, his family, the parties hosted, his parochial, commercial and electoral positions, and from there it was just a hop and a skip to the rumours and the anecdotes. João das Mercês's excellent memory retained all things, the greatest and the least, with such clarity that it was as if they had occurred on the previous day, and so completely that not even their own subjects could repeat them so impeccably. He knew them as well as he knew the Lord's Prayer, which is to say without having to think about the words; he prayed just as he ate, chewing on the prayer, which came out of his jaws without his feeling it. If the rules mandated the praying of three dozen Our Fathers in a row, João das Mercês would say them without even counting. So was he with other people's lives; he loved to know them, he researched them, memorised them, and never after would they leave his memory.

All in the parish loved him well because he neither meddled nor cursed. He had a love of art for art's sake. Often he had no need even to ask questions. José would tell him of Antônio's life and Antônio of José's. What he did was to ratify or rectify each by the other, and both of those with Sancho, Sancho with Martinho, and vice versa, everyone with everyone. And thus he filled his empty hours, which were many. Sometimes, at mass itself, he would recall some story from the night before, and, at first, he would ask God's forgiveness; then he stopped asking for it when he considered that he had not in fact got a single word or action of the Holy Sacrifice wrong, so consubstantiated did he carry them within him. The story that he was reanimating for a few moments was merely like the swallow flying across a landscape. The landscape is unchanged, and the water, if there is water, murmurs its same sound. This comparison, which was his own, was worth more than he realised, because the swallow, even in flight, makes up a part of the landscape, and the story made up a part of him as a person, it was one of his acts of living.

By the time he arrived at the comendador's house, he had unravelled the rosary of that man's life, and he entered right-foot first so as not to bring on any bad luck. He did not intend to leave early, distressing though the occasion might be, and in this respect fortune came to his aid. Brito was in the front parlour, in conversation with his wife, when he received notification that João das Mercês was asking after the condition of the two dying people. His wife withdrew, and the sacristan came in apologising and saying he wouldn't stay long, he was just passing and had thought to ask if the sick people had gone to heaven – or if they were still of this world. Anything the comendador might tell him on the subject he would hear with interest.

"They have not died, but nor do I know whether they will pull through, although she, at least, I believe will die," Brito concluded.

"They do seem in a very bad way."

"She especially; it is also she who suffers worse from the fever. The fever caught them here at our house, on their arrival from Campinas, some days ago."

"They were here already?" asked the sacristan, amazed not to have known this.

"They were; they arrived a fortnight ago, or thereabouts. They came with my nephew Carlos, and here they caught the sickness . . ."

Brito stopped in mid-speech; or so it seemed to the sacristan, who filled his face with the whole expression of a person waiting to hear the rest. However, since the other man was biting his lips and looking at the walls, he didn't notice the waiting gesture, and both remained silent. Brito ended up pacing the length of the room, while João das Mercês told himself that there was surely something here more than a fever. The first idea that came to him was that the doctors had made a mistake in the illness or the remedy; he also thought it might be some other hidden ailment, which they called fever so as to conceal the truth. His eyes were following the comendador, as the man walked up and down the whole length of the room, treading quietly so as not to disturb the people inside the house. Some murmurings of conversation were drifting in from there, a call, a message, a door opening or closing. All of this would have been nothing to a man who had other cares, but right now the sacristan's sole care was to know what he did not know. At least, the family of the sick couple, their position, their current condition, some episode from their lives, learning anything at all would be something, however far removed it might be from his parish.

"Oh!" exclaimed Brito, stopping short.

He seemed to have an impatient urge to recount an affair – the "terrible story" he had announced to the sacristan a little earlier; but one man dared not ask for it nor the other man speak it, and the comendador resumed his pacing.

João das Mercês sat down. He could see that in such a situation it would be most seemly to take his leave with some fine words of hope or comfort, and return the next day; but he preferred to sit and wait. He saw no sign of disapproval at his action in the other man's face; on the contrary, the comendador stopped before him and sighed very wearily.

"Sad, yes, sad," João das Mercês agreed. "Good people, are they not?"

"They were to have been married."

"Married? They were engaged to each other?"

Brito nodded an affirmative. The tone was melancholy, but there was no sign of the previously announced terrible story, and the sacristan waited for it. He remarked to himself that this was the first time ever that he was hearing anything about people he absolutely did not know at all. Their faces, seen not long before, were the only sign he had of these people. Not that this made him any less curious. They were to have been married ... Perhaps that itself was the terrible story. Truly, assailed by a sickness on the eve of such goodness, the ill must perforce be a terrible one. Engaged and dying ...

Somebody came in with a message for the owner of the house; he excused himself to the sacristan, so quickly that the other man did not even have time to say goodbye and leave. He ran inside, and remained there for fifty minutes. Then, a muffled weeping reached the room; straight after this, the comendador returned.

"What was I saying to you, a short while back? That she, at least, would die; she has died."

Brito said this without tears and almost without sadness. He had not known the deceased woman long.

The tears, by his account, were those of his nephew from Campinas and a kinswoman of the deceased, who lived in Mata-porcos. To progress from that information to supposing that the comendador's nephew was in love with the dying man's fiancée took the sacristan barely a moment, but he did not hold the idea for long; it was not necessarily so, and after all, this nephew had accompanied them himself . . . Perhaps he was to have been their best man. He wanted to know – and this was quite natural – the name of the deceased. The owner of the house – either not wanting to give it to him, or because another idea entered his head now – did not state the name of the bride-to-be, nor of her fiancé. Perhaps for both reasons.

"They were due to marry . . ."

"God will receive her into his holy care, and him too, if he should die," said the sacristan with the greatest melancholy.

And these words were enough to drag out half of the secret that seemed so eager to emerge from the ship-provisioner's mouth. When João das Mercês saw the expression in his eyes, the gesture with which he called him over to the window, and the promise that he made him swear – he swore on all the souls of his kin that he would listen to everything and keep silent about everything. And he was not a man to spread other people's confidences, especially those of men as important and esteemed as the comendador. At which the other man seemed satisfied, and encouraged, and he confided the first part of the secret to him, which was that the engaged couple, raised together, had come to marry here when they had learned, from the relative in Mata-porcos, a frightful piece of news . . .

"Which was?" João das Mercês said hurriedly, sensing some hesitation on the comendador's part.

"That they were brother and sister."

"How so, brother and sister? You mean, actual siblings?"

"Actual siblings, by their mother. It was their father who was not the same. The relative did not explain it all to them clearly, but she swore that this was so, and they were devastated for a day or more . . ."

João das Mercês was no less amazed than they had been; he resolved not to leave that place until he had learned the rest. He heard the clocks strike ten, he would hear all the other hours of the night, too, he would sit watch with one or both bodies, so long as he could add this page to the others of the parish, even if it was not of the parish.

"And go on, do go on, it was then that the fever took them . . .?"

Brito clenched his teeth so as to say no more. Since, however, he had been summoned inside again, he responded quickly and half an hour later he was back, with the report of the second passing. The weeping, which was more open now, though more expected, there being nobody from whom to hide it, had brought the news to the sacristan.

"There the other has gone, the brother, the fiancé . . . May God forgive them. You should know it all now, my friend. You should know that they so loved each other that a few days after learning the impediment, in nature and in canon law, to their partnership, they resolved, being only half-siblings and not full siblings, to board a cabriolet and run away from home. The alarm being quickly raised, the cabriolet was apprehended on the road to Cidade Nova, and they were so angry and distressed at being caught that they fell sick with a fever and they have just died."

It is impossible to describe how the sacristan felt, on hearing this story. He kept it to himself for some time, difficult though this was. He learned the people's names from the obituary in the newspapers, and combined the circumstances he had learned from the comendador with some others. In short, without ever feeling too indiscreet, he spread the story around, just disguising the names and telling it to one friend, who passed it to another, and this one to others still, and so from everyone to everyone. He did more than this: he got it into his head that the cabriolet of their flight might have been the same as that of the last rites; he went to the coach house, chatted casually with a man working there, and learned that it was. Hence this story's coming to be called the "tale of the cabriolet".

THE STICK

D AMIÃO RAN AWAY from the seminary at eleven
in the morning, one Friday in August. I am not
certain of the year, but it was before 1850. After a few
minutes, he stopped, troubled; he had not expected to
see the expression in others' eyes as this young seminarian rushed past them looking so surprised, fearful,
fugitive. He was unfamiliar with the streets, he kept
needing to retrace his steps, and finally he just stopped.
Where was he to go? Not home, no, there awaited his
father, who would send him straight back to the seminary, after a sound punishment. He had not fixed
upon his place of refuge, because his departure had
been set for some later time; only a chance circumstance had hastened it. Where to go? He remembered
his godfather, João Carneiro, but his godfather was a
weak-willed sluggard of a man, who of his own voli-
tion would never do anything useful. It had been he
who had taken Damião to the seminary and

introduced him to the rector: I bring you the great man he is to become, he had said.

"Come in," the rector replied, "come in, great man, always providing that you are also modest and good. True greatness is humble. So, young man . . ."

That was his arrival. Not long afterwards, the lad fled the seminary. And now we encounter him here on the streets, afraid, unsure, finding neither refuge nor counsel; he ran through all the houses of relatives and friends in his memory, but settled on none of them. All of a sudden, he exclaimed:

"I shall appeal to Mistress Rita! She will send for my godfather, and tell him that she wants me to leave the seminary . . . Maybe in that way . . ."

Mistress Rita was a widow, beloved of João Carneiro; Damião had some vague sense of the situation and tried to take advantage of it. Where did she live? He was in such a daze that within minutes he was at her house; it was on the Largo do Capim.

"Holy Name of Jesus! What is this?" shouted Mistress Rita, sitting up from the cane-seat sofa on which she had been reclining.

Damião had just burst in, terrified; the moment he arrived at the house, he had seen a priest going by, and gave the door a shove, finding it by good fortune neither locked nor bolted. Once inside he peered through the spyhole, to watch the priest. The man did not notice him and went on walking.

"But what is this, Senhor Damião?" the lady of the house cried again, only now recognising him. "What are you doing here?"

Damião, trembling, barely able to speak, told her not to be afraid, it was nothing; he would explain it all.

"Calm yourself; and do explain."

"I shall tell you right away; I have committed no crime, I swear it, but wait."

Mistress Rita looked at him in astonishment, and the girls, both those from that household and those from outside, who were all sitting around the room before their lacework cushions, brought the bobbins and their hands to a stop. Mistress Rita lived mostly off teaching lacework, as well as drawn threadwork and embroidery.

While the lad caught his breath, she ordered the girls to get back to their task, and waited. Finally, Damião told her everything, how unhappy the seminary had made him, how he was sure he could never make a good priest; he spoke passionately, and he asked her to save him.

"How so? There is nothing I can do."

"You could, if you wished."

"No," she replied, shaking her head, "I do not interfere in your family's business, I hardly know them; and that father of yours, they say he has quite a temper!"

Damião saw that he was lost. He kneeled at her feet, kissed her hands, desperate.

"You could do so much, Mistress Rita; I beg you, for the love of God, by all you hold most sacred, by your husband's soul, save me from death, for I shall kill myself if I am compelled to return to that place."

Mistress Rita, flattered by the lad's entreaties, tried to call him back to other feelings. The life of a priest was holy and beautiful, she told him; time would show him that it was better to overcome his aversions and one day . . . No, nothing of the sort, never!, Damião retorted, shaking his head and kissing her hands, and repeating that it would be his death. Mistress Rita hesitated another long while, finally asking why he had not gone to his godfather.

"My godfather? He is even worse than Father; he doesn't listen to me, I suspect he doesn't listen to anybody . . ."

"He doesn't listen?" Mistress Rita interrupted him, her pride wounded. "Oh, we'll see if he listens or not . . ."

She called over a slave boy and commanded him to go to Senhor João Carneiro's house and summon him at once; and if he did not find him at home, he was to ask where he might be found, and run to tell him that she dearly needed to speak with him, and right away.

"Go, boy."

Damião gave a loud, sad sigh. She, to cover up the authoritative way in which she had given those orders, explained to the youth that Senhor João Carneiro had been a friend of her husband's, and that he had found a few girls for her to teach. Then, since he was still looking sad, leaning against a doorway, she tweaked his nose, laughing:

"Oh, come now, little priestling, you can rest easy, everything will be resolved."

Mistress Rita was forty years old by her baptismal certificate, and twenty-seven in her eyes. She was personable, lively, jovial, quick to laugh; but when it suited her, as fierce as any devil. She wanted to cheer the boy up, and despite the circumstances, she did not find this particularly hard. Soon enough, both were laughing, she was telling him amusing stories, and asking for others in return, which he related with a singular charm. One of them, a most foolish story, which required the pulling of funny faces, made one of Mistress Rita's girls laugh, forgetting her work, because she was looking at and listening to the lad.

Mistress Rita picked up a stick that was beside the sofa, and threatened her:

"Lucrécia, better watch out for the stick!"

The little girl lowered her head, meaning to ward off the blow, but the blow did not come. It was a warning; if at nightfall her task was not completed, Lucrécia would receive the usual punishment. Damião looked at the child; she was a little black girl, skinny, a scrap of nothing, with a scar on her forehead and a burn on her left hand. She was eleven years old. Damião noticed that she was coughing, but inwardly, mutely, so as not to interrupt the conversation. He was sorry for the girl and resolved to give her his protection if she did not complete her work. Mistress Rita would not deny him the pardon . . . Besides, the girl had laughed because she found him funny; it had been his fault, if being funny should be the cause for blame.

At this point, João Carneiro arrived. He went pale when he saw his godson, and looked at Mistress Rita, who wasted no time on preamble. She told him that the lad needed to be removed from the seminary, that he had no vocation for the ecclesiastical life, and better to have one fewer priest than a bad one. He could love and serve Our Lord out here, too. João Carneiro, astonished, could think of no reply for the first few minutes; finally, he opened his mouth and reprimanded his godson for having come to trouble "strangers", and declared at once that he would be punished.

"Punished? Nonsense!" Mistress Rita interrupted him. "Punish him for what? Go, go talk to your godson's father."

"Well, I can make no guarantees, I do not believe it will be possible . . ."

"It must be possible, I myself guarantee it. If you want it, senhor," she went on with a rather suggestive note to her voice, "I have no doubt that all will be resolved. And do press him, to make him yield. Go, Senhor João Carneiro, your godson shall not return to the seminary; I am telling you he will not go back . . ."

"But my dear senhora . . ."

"Go on, go."

João Carneiro could not bring himself to leave, but neither could he stay. He was torn between two opposing forces. It did not trouble him when all was said and done if the boy ended up a cleric, a lawyer or a doctor, or some other thing entirely, a vagrant even, but the worst was that he himself was being committed to a tremendous struggle with his old friend's most personal feelings, with no certainty of the result; and if it proved negative, another struggle with Mistress Rita, whose final words had been threatening: "I am telling you he will not go back." There would of necessity be a scandal. João Carneiro's pupils were wild, his eyelids flickering, his chest heaving. The looks that he cast upon Mistress Rita were looks of entreaty, mixed with a thin flash of censure. Why had she not asked him for some other thing? Why had she not ordered him to go, on foot, in the rain, to Tijuca or Jacarepaguá? But to persuade his friend to change his son's career . . . He knew the old man; he was quite capable of smashing a jug over his head. Oh! If only the lad could drop down there, all of a sudden, apoplectic, dead! That would be a solution – a cruel one, no question, but quite final.

"Well?" Mistress Rita insisted.

He gestured with his hand that she should wait. He was scratching his beard, trying to find some other recourse. God in Heaven! A papal decree dissolving the Church, or, at least, wiping out seminaries, would bring everything to a satisfactory end, João Carneiro would return home and sit down to a game of *tresette*. Imagine Napoleon's barber being tasked with leading the battle of Austerlitz . . . But the Church was still there, and seminaries were still there, and his godson was still affixed to the wall, eyes downcast as he waited, offering no apoplectic solution.

"Go, go," said Mistress Rita, handing him his hat and his cane.

There was no alternative. The barber put his razor back into its case, buckled on his sword and sallied forth to battle. Damião took a deep breath; his outward appearance was unchanged, eyes pinned to the floor, dejected. This time, Mistress Rita tweaked his chin.

"Go have your dinner, enough moping."

"Do you really think, senhora, he will manage to do anything?"

"He will manage to do everything," Mistress Rita retorted, full of herself. "Go, the soup is getting cold." In spite of Mistress Rita's playful nature, and his own natural light-heartedness, Damião was less cheerful at dinner than he had been when the day began. He did not trust his godfather's weak character. Nevertheless, he dined well; and, by the end of the meal, he was back to the morning's joking. During dessert, he heard the noise of people from the living-room, and asked if they had come to take him away.

"That must be the young ladies."

They got up from the table and walked over to the living-room. The young ladies were five women from the neighbourhood who came every afternoon to take coffee with Mistress Rita, and remained there until nightfall.

Her pupils, their dinner concluded, returned to work on their cushions. Mistress Rita presided over this whole

79

crowd of womenfolk from the household and from outside. The whispering of the bobbins and the chattering of the young women echoed in a way that was so earthly, so remote from theology and Latin, that the boy surrendered to them and forgot all else. For the first few minutes, there was still a little shyness on the part of the neighbourhood women, but it soon passed. One of them sang a modinha, accompanied on the guitar, which was plucked by Mistress Rita, and the afternoon sped past. Before it was over, Mistress Rita asked Damião to tell one specific funny story that had greatly pleased her. It was the one that had made Lucrécia laugh.

"Go on, Senhor Damião, don't you start being coy now, these young women are eager to head off home. You will all like it very much."

Damião had no choice but to obey. Despite the introduction and the sense of expectation, which served to reduce the joke and its effect, the story concluded to laughter from the young women. Damião, quite pleased with himself, had not forgotten Lucrécia, and he looked over at her to see if she too was laughing. She had her head bent over her cushion to finish her task. She was not laughing; or if she was, she was laughing inwardly, the way she coughed.

The neighbours all left, and the evening fell for good. Damião's soul was turning gloomy, along with the night. What could be happening? Every moment, he would go to peer through the spyhole, returning more disheartened each time. No trace of his godfather. Surely his father had silenced him, then had called for two slaves, gone to the police to request an officer, and come to take him by force and return him to the seminary. Damião asked Mistress Rita if the house did not have a back door; he ran out to the yard and judged that he should be able to jump the wall. He also wondered if there was any way of escaping down Rua da Vala, or if it would be better to see whether some neighbour might be so kind as to take him in. The worst part of it was the cassock; if Mistress Rita could get hold of an old redingote, a frock coat . . . Mistress Rita did indeed have a frock coat available, a piece left forgotten by João Carneiro, or a remembrance of his.

"I do have a coat of my late husband's," she laughed, "but why all these alarms? Everything will surely be resolved, you can rest easy."

Finally, at nightfall, one of his godfather's slaves appeared, with a letter for Mistress Rita. The business was not yet settled; his father had been furious and wanted to smash everything up; he had shouted oh no senhor, and that the naughty child would have to go to the seminary, otherwise he would have him locked up in the Aljube or sent to the prison ship. João Carneiro had fought for some time to prevent his godson's father from making up his mind right away, to get him to sleep on it, and think hard about whether it was appropriate to hand over to religion a fellow who was so rebellious and immoral. He explained in the letter that he had said this in the better hope of prevailing in their cause. He did not consider the battle won, but the following day he meant to return to his friend, and insist again. He concluded by saying that the youth should go to his house.

Damião finished reading the letter and looked at Mistress Rita. I have no other resort, he thought. Mistress Rita sent for an inkhorn, and on the reverse of the same letter she wrote this reply: "My dear Joãozinho, either you save the boy or we never see each other again." She sealed the letter with a wafer, and handed it to the slave, instructing him to convey it in haste. She went back to cheering up the seminarian, who was once again shrouded beneath a hood of humility and dismay. She told him to settle down, that the matter was hers now.

"They will have to see what I am good for. Oh, do not think I jest!"

The time had come to gather up the pieces of work. Mistress Rita examined them; all of the pupils had concluded their tasks. Only Lucrécia was still at her cushion, working the bobbins, no longer able to see. Mistress Rita walked over to her, saw that the job was not yet done, became furious and grabbed her by an ear.

"Oh! You little rascal!"

"Oh mistress, oh! For the love of God! By Our Lady in Heaven."

"Wretch! Our Lady does not protect layabouts!"

Lucrécia yanked herself away, managing to escape the lady's hands, and fled inside; the lady followed and grabbed hold of her.

"Come here!"

"Oh, please, my senhora, forgive me!"

"No – I will not."

And both returned to the living-room, one of them led by the ear, struggling, crying and entreating; the other saying no, that she needed to be punished.

"Where is the stick?"

The stick was at the head of the sofa, on the other side of the living-room. Mistress Rita, not wanting to let go of the girl, shouted to the seminarian:

"Senhor Damião, hand me that stick, if you would be so kind?"

Damião froze . . . Oh, cruel moment! A cloud passed in front of his eyes. Yes, he had sworn to protect the girl, whose work had been delayed on his account . . .

"Give me the stick, Senhor Damião!"

Damião did walk towards the sofa. Then the little black girl begged him by everything holy, by his mother, by his father, by Our Lord himself . . .

"Help me, master young-man sir!"

Mistress Rita, her face aflame and eyes bulging, insisted upon the stick, never letting go of the little black girl, who was now caught in a fit of coughing. Damião felt some remorse; but he did so need to get out of the seminary! He came to the sofa, took up the stick and handed it to Mistress Rita.

THE SECRET CAUSE

GARCIA, STANDING, WAS looking at his finger-nails and clicking them; Fortunato, in the rocking-chair, was staring at the ceiling; Maria Luísa, sitting by the window, was finishing up a piece of needlework. For the last five minutes, nobody had spoken. They had already talked about the day, which was very fine; about Catumbi, where Fortunato and his wife lived; and about a private hospital, which will be explained in due course. Since the three characters present are now dead and buried, the time has come to tell this story unvarnished.

They had talked about another matter, too, apart from those three, something so grim and serious that it did not leave them much of a taste for discussing the weather, the neighbourhood and the hospital. The whole conversation on that matter was uncomfortable. Right now, Maria Luísa's fingers seem still to be trembling, while Garcia's face wears a severe expression that is not habitual. In truth, what had happened was of such a nature that to understand it requires a return to the origins of the situation.

Garcia had graduated, in medicine, the previous year, 1861. In 1860, while still a student, he had met Fortunato, for the first time, at the door of the Santa Casa hospital; he was going in as the other man was coming out. He was rather struck by this figure; even so, he would have forgotten him, had it not been for their second encounter, a few days later. He lived on the Rua de Dom Manoel. One of his rare distractions was going to the São Januário theatre, which was nearby, between that street and the beach; he went once or twice a month, and never found more than forty people there. Only the most intrepid dared to venture into that corner of the city. One night, when Garcia had already taken his chair, Fortunato appeared and took a seat beside him.

The play was a melodrama, stitched together roughly out of stabbings, enlivened with curses and remorse; but Fortunato listened with singular interest. At the more painful moments, his attention was redoubled, his eyes would move greedily from one character to another, to the point where the student suspected that the play contained certain of his neighbour's personal reminiscences. When the drama came to an end, there was a farce; but Fortunato did not wait to see it and left; Garcia followed him. Fortunato made his way down the Beco do Cotovelo, the Rua de São José, to the Largo da Carioca. He was walking slowly, head down, stopping occasionally to whack some sleeping dog with his cane; the dog would be left yelping and the man walked on. At the Largo da Carioca he got into a tilbury, and headed off towards Praça da Constituição. Garcia returned home having learned no more.

A few weeks went by. One night, it was nine o'clock, he was at home, when he heard the sound of voices on the stairs; he immediately came down from the attic, where he lived, to the first floor, which was home to a man who worked at the military arsenal. It was this man who was being led by a few others, up the stairs, bleeding. His black servant came to open the door; Garcia's neighbour was moaning, the voices were confused, the light poor. Once the injured man had been set down on his bed, Garcia said that a doctor should be called.

"One is on his way," somebody replied.

Garcia turned to look: it was the very same man from the Santa Casa and the theatre. He imagined this must be a relative or friend of the victim's; but he rejected the presumption when he heard him ask whether the man had any family or somebody who was close. The black servant told him no, and the stranger took on the directing of affairs, asked all the others to withdraw, paid the carriers, and gave preliminary instructions. On learning that Garcia was his neighbour and a medical student, he asked him to stay to assist the doctor. Then he told him what had happened.

"It was a gang of capoeiras. I was coming from the Moura barracks, where I had been visiting a cousin, when I heard a very loud noise, and straight after that a scuffle. Seems they also wounded another fellow who was passing by, and who disappeared down one of those alleyways; but I saw only this gentleman, who was just crossing the street when one of the capoeiras, brushing past, stuck his dagger into him. He didn't fall at once; he told me where he lived, and since it was only a couple of steps away, I thought it best to bring him here."

"Did you know him?" Garcia asked.

"No, I've never seen him before. Who is he?"

"He's a fine man, works at the military arsenal. By the name of Gouvêa."

"I don't know him."

Doctor and police officer arrived shortly afterwards; they dressed the wound, and took down some details. The stranger said that his name was Fortunato Gomes da Silveira, that he was a capitalist, a bachelor, resident of Catumbi. The wound was deemed serious. While it was being bandaged up, with the student's aid, Fortunato acted as servant, holding the basin, the candle, the cloths, disturbing nothing, looking coolly at the injured man, who was moaning a great deal. At the end, he had some private conference with the doctor, walked him to the landing, and reiterated to the officer his statement of willingness to assist in the police enquiries. The two men left, and Fortunato and the student remained behind in the room.

Garcia was amazed. He watched Fortunato sit down calmly, stretch out his legs, put his hands in his trouser pockets and stare at the wounded man. His eyes were light, the colour of lead, they moved slowly, and had a look in them that was hard, dry and cold. His face was thin and pale; a narrow strip of beard, running under his chin and from one temple to the other, short, red and sparse. He must have been forty. From time to time, he would turn to the student and ask him something about the wounded man; but he would quickly go back to looking at Gouvêa, while the youth gave his answer. The sensation that the student gleaned was of revulsion and simultaneously of curiosity; he could not deny that he was witnessing an act of uncommon dedication, and that if the man were as disinterested as he seemed, then there was nothing for it but simply to accept the human heart as a well of mysteries.

Fortunato left a little before one; he returned in the days that followed, but the cure proceeded quickly, and before it was over, he disappeared without telling the beneficiary of his kindness where he lived. It was the student who supplied his name, street and number.

"I will thank him for the charity he did me, as soon as I can leave the house," the convalescing man said.

He hurried to Catumbi six days later. Fortunato received him with some awkwardness, he heard his words of thanks impatiently, gave him a bored reply and ended up tapping his knee with the tassels of his robe. Gouvêa, who was sitting opposite him, wordless, smoothed his hat down with his fingers, looking up occasionally, unable to find anything more to say. After ten minutes, he excused himself, and left.

"Watch out for the capoeiras!" said the master of the house, laughing.

The poor devil left the place mortified, humiliated, painfully chewing over the man's scorn, struggling to forget it, to explain it or to forgive it, in order that his heart might retain only the memory of the good deed; but his efforts were in vain. Resentment, a new and exclusive guest, came in to expel the act of kindness, a scoundrel climbing into his head to take refuge there as a simple idea. Thus it was the benefactor himself who instilled in this man a feeling of ingratitude.

All this amazed Garcia. This young man possessed, in embryonic form, the skill of deciphering men, of breaking down their natures, he was a lover of analysis, and he felt the pleasure, which he considered supreme, of penetrating many spiritual layers, until he could touch a creature's deepest secret. His curiosity piqued, he thought to pay a call on the man from Catumbi, but realised that he had not even received a formal invitation to the house. He needed some pretext at least, and he could find none.

Sometime later, when he had already graduated and was living on the Rua de Matacavalos, close to the Rua do Conde, he ran into Fortunato in an omnibus, and he met him several other times, too, and this frequency brought a certain familiarity. One day, Fortunato invited Garcia to pay him a visit nearby, in Catumbi.

"Did you know that I am married?"

"I did not."

"I married four months ago, though I could swear it was four days. Come dine with us on Sunday."

"Sunday?"

"Do not struggle to devise some excuse; I will accept none. Come on Sunday."

Garcia went on Sunday. Fortunato gave him a good dinner, good cigars and good conversation, in the company of his wife, an interesting woman. His appearance had not changed; his eyes were the same plates of tin, hard and cold; his other features were no more attractive than they had been before. His kindnesses, however, if they did not redeem his nature, did offer some not inconsiderable compensation. Maria Luísa, meanwhile, possessed both charms, in person and in manner. She was slender, graceful, her eyes sweet and docile; she was twenty-five and seemed no older than nineteen. Garcia noticed, on his second visit, that there was between them some dissonance of character, little or no moral affinity, and from wife towards husband a manner that transcended respect and verged on resignation and fear. One day, when the three of them were together, Garcia asked Maria Luísa whether she had heard the circumstances in which he first became acquainted with her husband.

"No," the young woman replied.

"Then you shall hear a fine deed."

"It is not worth the telling," Fortunato interrupted him.

"You will see for yourself, senhora, whether it is worth it," the doctor insisted.

He relayed the story from the Rua de Dom Manoel. The young woman listened, amazed. Unthinkingly she reached out and squeezed her husband's wrist, smiling and appreciative, as if she had just discovered his heart. Fortunato shrugged, but he, too, was listening not indifferently. When it was over, he himself described the visit that the wounded man had paid him, with every detail of his appearance, his gestures, his awkward words, all the silences: in short, such an utter fool. And he laughed a great deal as he described it. It was not the laugh of duplicity. Duplicity is evasive and sidelong; his laugh was cheerful and open.

"A most rare man!" thought Garcia.

Maria Luísa was quite downcast at her husband's mockery; but the doctor restored her to her former contentment, referring once again to his devotion and his uncommon qualities as a nurse; such a good nurse, he concluded, that if ever I were to set up a hospital, I would invite him to be a part of it.

"Well, shall we?" asked Fortunato.

"Shall we what?"

"Shall we set up a hospital?"

"No, we shall not; I spoke in jest."

"Something might well be done; and for you, senhor, seeing as you are just starting out in your practice, I think it would be very good indeed. I do in fact have a house that will be vacant, and it would suit well enough."

Garcia said no on that day and on the next; but the idea had lodged itself in the other man's head, and he could back down no more. In truth, it was indeed a good way for him to introduce himself, and it could prove good business for them both. He finally accepted, some days later, which was a disappointment for Maria Luísa. A nervous, fragile thing, she suffered at the mere idea that her husband should be constantly in contact with human illnesses, but she dared not oppose him, and bowed her head. The plan was made and carried out quickly. The fact is that Fortunato attended to nothing else, not then, nor later. Once the establishment was open, he himself was its administrator and head nurse, he examined everything, arranged everything, the purchases and broths, drugs and invoices.

Garcia was now able to confirm that the attention paid to the wounded man from Rua de Dom Manoel had not been a mere chance event, but was rooted in this man's very nature. He saw him do more service than any servant. There was nothing from which he recoiled, no disease was too distressing or repellent, and he was always ready for anything, at any hour of the day or night. Everybody marvelled and applauded. Fortunato studied, observed the operations, and nobody else administered the caustics.

"I have great faith in caustics," he would say.

The communion of their interests tightened the bonds of intimacy. Garcia became a regular presence in the house; he dined there almost every day; there he observed the person and life of Maria Luísa, whose spiritual solitude was quite evident. And this solitude seemed somehow to double her charm. Garcia started to feel something unsettle him whenever she appeared, when she talked, when she worked, silently, beside the window, or when she took to the piano to play sad songs. Gently, gently, love entered his heart. When he noticed it, he wanted to expel it so that there should be nothing binding him and Fortunato but friendship; but he could not do it. He could only lock it away; Maria Luísa understood both things, the affection and the silence, but feigned ignorance.

At the beginning of October, an incident took place that further opened the doctor's eyes to the young woman's situation. Fortunato had taken to studying anatomy and physiology, and filled his free hours cutting open cats and dogs and poisoning them. As the animals' squeals were distressing the patients, he moved his laboratory into his home, and it was his wife, though nervous in constitution, who had to endure them. One day, however, unable to bear any more, she went to the doctor and asked him, as a favour to her, to secure from her husband an end to such experiments.

"But you yourself, senhora . . ."

Maria Luísa replied, smiling:

"He will naturally think me a child. What I would like is for you, senhor, as a doctor, to tell him that I suffer by it; and please believe that I do . . ."

It did not take Garcia long to persuade the other man to put a stop to those investigations. If he continued to practise them somewhere else, nobody knew it, but it is possible. Maria Luísa thanked the doctor, for her own sake as well as for the animals', whom she could not bear to see suffer. She coughed occasionally; Garcia asked if anything ailed her, and she replied that it was nothing.

"Let me check your pulse."

"I am quite well."

She did not give him her wrist, and withdrew. Garcia was apprehensive. He supposed, on the contrary, that there might be something the matter with her, that he needed to observe her and warn her husband in time.

Two days later – the very day on which we find them now – Garcia went to their house to dine. In the living-room, he was informed that Fortunato was in his study, and he walked over there; he was just approaching the door, when Maria Luísa emerged in distress.

"What is the matter?" he asked.

"The mouse! The mouse!" exclaimed the young woman, choked, hurrying away.

Garcia recalled hearing Fortunato complain the previous day about a mouse that had carried off some important piece of paper; but he never could have expected what he saw. He saw Fortunato seated at the table in the middle of the study, on which he had placed a dish of aqua vitae. The liquid blazed. Between his left thumb and index finger he was holding a piece of twine, and from its end the mouse was hanging by its tail. In his right hand, he had a pair of scissors. At the moment Garcia entered, Fortunato was cutting off one of the mouse's legs; then he brought the unfortunate creature down to the flame, quickly, so as not to kill it, and readied himself to do the same with the third leg, the first having been cut off previously. Garcia stopped dead, appalled.

"Kill it right away!" he said.

"Soon enough."

And with a most unusual smile, the reflection of a soul satisfied, something that conveyed his private pleasure as the highest of sensations, Fortunato cut off the mouse's third leg and for the third time made the same movement towards the flame. The wretched creature writhed, squealing, bloody, scorched, and did not finally die. Garcia looked away, then looked back again, and held out his hand to prevent the torture from continuing, but he was prevented, because the devil of a man inspired fear, with that radiant serenity in his face. The last leg was yet to be cut off; Fortunato cut it very slowly, his eyes following the scissors; the leg dropped off, and he kept his eyes on the half-corpse mouse. As he brought it down for the fourth time, into the flame, he made the gesture even quicker, to preserve, if he could, a few shreds of life.

Garcia, standing opposite him, managed to master his revulsion at the spectacle to look closely at the man's face. No rage, and no hatred; nothing but a vast pleasure, still and profound, such as another man might exhibit on hearing a beautiful sonata or seeing a divine statue, something like a pure aesthetic feeling. He thought, and it was true, that Fortunato had entirely forgotten him. If that was so, he would not be feigning, and this really must be the case. The flame was dying away, the mouse might still have a last trace of life in it, the shadow of a shadow; Fortunato took advantage of this to cut off its snout and for the last time to bring its flesh to the fire. Finally he dropped the body into the dish, and pushed this whole mixture of singeing and blood away.

As he stood, he noticed the doctor and gave a start. Then he showed some anger towards the mouse, which had eaten his piece of paper; but his rage was clearly feigned.

"He punishes without anger," thought the doctor, "out of the need to find a feeling of pleasure, which only another's pain can provide: that is this man's secret."

Fortunato exaggerated his claim about how important the paper had been, the loss that it had caused him, a loss of time, certainly, but time was hugely precious to him now. Garcia just listened, not saying a word, and not believing him. He remembered the man's actions, the serious ones and the light ones, and found the same explanation for them all. It was the same change to the keys of his sensibility, a *sui generis* dilettantism, Caligula in miniature.

When Maria Luísa returned to the study soon afterwards, her husband went to her, laughing; he took her hands and spoke to her gently:

"Poor little weakling!"

And turning to the doctor:

"Can you believe she almost fainted?"

Maria Luísa defended her fearfulness, saying that she was nervous and a woman; then she went to sit at the window with her wools and her needles, fingers still trembling, just as we saw them at the start of this story. It should be recalled that, after having spoken of other things, the three of them remained silent, the husband seated and staring up at the ceiling, the doctor clicking his nails. A short while later, they went in to dine; but the meal was not a happy one. Maria Luísa brooded and coughed; the doctor wondered if she might not have exposed herself to some sort of excess in the company of such a man. It was only possible; but love transformed the possibility into a certainty; he trembled for her and took care to keep an eye on them both.

She coughed, she coughed, and it was not long before the illness showed its face. It was consumption, that insatiable old dame who sucks out all your life until she has left nothing but a husk of bones. Fortunato received the news like a blow; he truly loved his wife, in his way, he was used to her, it would be hard for him to lose her. He spared no efforts, doctors, medicines, changes of air, every resource and every palliative. But it was all in vain. The illness was deadly.

In the young woman's final days, in the presence of her greatest torments, her husband's nature subdued any other feeling. He did not leave her side; he settled his dull cold eye on the slow, painful decomposition of life, he drank in one by one the afflictions of this lovely creature, now so thin and transparent, consumed by fever and undermined by death. The harshest selfishness, hungry for sensations, could not spare him a single moment of her agony, nor did he pay for it with a single tear, whether in public or in private. It was only when she died that he was stunned. Coming around, he found that he was once again alone.

That night, when a kinswoman of Maria Luísa's, who had helped her to die, had gone to take some rest, Fortunato and Garcia were left in the living-room, keeping watch over the body, both lost in thought; but the husband was tired, and the doctor told him that he ought to rest a little.

"Go, take a nap for an hour or two: I will go later."

Fortunato left, he went to lie on the sofa in the adjacent parlour, and fell asleep right away. Twenty minutes later he awoke, wanted to go back to sleep, dozed for a few minutes, before getting up and returning to the living-room. He walked on tiptoes so as not to wake his wife's relative, who was sleeping nearby. When he reached the door, he stopped short, astonished.

Garcia had walked over to the body, lifted the sheet and gazed for a few moments at the extinguished features. Then, as if death spiritualised everything, he leaned in and kissed her forehead. This was the moment Fortunato reached the doorway. He stopped short, astonished; this could not be the kiss of friendship, it might rather be the epilogue of an adulterous novel. Please note, he was not jealous; nature had formed him such that he felt no jealousy nor envy, but it had given him vanity, which is no less a prisoner to resentment.

He looked stunned, chewing on his lips.

Meanwhile, Garcia bent over again to kiss the corpse once again; but then he could bear no more. The kiss broke into sobs, and his eyes could not contain their tears, which gushed out, tears of unspoken love, and incurable despair. Fortunato, at the door, where he had remained, calmly savoured this explosion of moral pain that was so long, so very, deliciously long.

THE CANON
OR METAPHYSICS OF STYLE

"Come with me from Lebanon, my bride, come from Lebanon . . . The mandrakes give forth their fragrance. At our doors are every kind of dove . . ."

"I conjure ye, oh daughters of Jerusalem, if ye find my beloved, give him to know how sick I am with love . . ."

Thus, to that melody from the ancient drama of Judah, in Canon Matias's head a noun and an adjective were searching for each other. Do not interrupt me, o hasty reader; I know you cannot believe a word I have to say. Yet say it I shall, in despite of your lack of faith, for the day of public conversion will come.

On that day – around 2222, I believe – the paradox will strip off its wings to don the heavy jacket of a simple truth. And then will this page deserve, not mere favour, but true apotheosis. It will be translated into every language. The academies and institutes will make a small book of it, for the use of the ages, bronze pages, gilt edging, letters of inlaid opal, and a matte silver cover. Governments will decree that it be taught at middle schools and high schools. The academies of philosophy will burn every preceding doctrine, even the most definitive, and embrace this new psychology, this sole truth, and all will be ended. Until that time, I will be made to look a fool, as you shall see.

Matias, honorary canon and working preacher, was composing a sermon when the psychic idyll began. He is forty years of age, and lives surrounded by books and books, somewhere around Gamboa. He has just received a commission for the sermon for some upcoming feast day; he, who had been relishing a great spiritual work, which had come in on the most recent steamship, turned the task down; but they were so insistent that he accepted.

"Your most high Reverence might do this in your sleep," said the organiser of the celebration.

Matias gave a smile that was gentle and discreet, the very way clergymen and diplomats ought to smile. The feasters bade him adieu with great gestures of veneration and went off to announce the event in the newspapers, with a statement that the gospel was to be preached by Canon Matias, "one of the adornments of the Brazilian clergy". This "adornment of the clergy" quite robbed the canon of his appetite for lunch when he read it this morning; and it was only for the sermon's having been agreed upon already that he set about writing it.

He began with ill will, but within a few minutes he is already working with love. Inspiration, with eyes to heaven, and meditation, with eyes cast down to the floor, perch on either side of his chair, whispering a thousand mystical and serious things into the canon's ear. Matias keeps on writing, now slowly, now quickly. The lines stream from his hands, lively and polished. Some require a few corrections or none at all. Suddenly, about to write down an adjective, he pauses; he writes another and strikes it out; yet another, which encounters no greater fortune. This is the crux of the idyll. Let us go up into the canon's head.

Hup! And here we are. That was not easy, was it, my dear reader? Just so you don't go believing those people who climb the Corcovado and say that the impression from its great height is such that man seems like nothing at all. An opinion that is panicked and false, as false as Judas and other diamonds. Oh, believe it not, beloved reader. No Corcovados, no Himalayas can compare to your head, which measures them. So here we are. Take a good look inside the canon's head.

We have the two brain hemispheres to choose from; but we are bound for this one, where nouns are born. Adjectives are born in the left. A discovery of mine, which is still not the main one, but is at its foundations, as you shall see. Yes, senhor, adjectives are born from one side, and nouns from the other, and every kind of word is divided in this way according to sexual difference . . .

"Sexual?"

Oh yes, my dear senhora, sexual. Words have sexes. I am just concluding my great psycholexicological memoirs, in which I explain and demonstrate this discovery. Words have a sex.

"So do they love one another?"

They do love one another. And they marry. Their marriage is what we call style. Please, my dear senhora, admit that you haven't understood a thing.

"I'll admit it, I haven't."

In that case, you, too, should join us in the canon's head. They are in fact sighing on this side. Do you know who it is that's sighing? It is that noun from earlier, the one the canon wrote on his piece of paper, when he suspended his nib. He is calling for just the right adjective, which will not come to him: "Come with me from Lebanon, come . . ." And this is how he speaks, since he is in the head of a priest; if this were a secular brain, the language would be Romeo's: "Juliet is the sun . . . arise, fair sun." But in an ecclesiastical head, the language is that of the Scriptures. Ultimately, what do the formulations matter? Lovers from Verona or lovers from Judah all speak in the same tongue, as is the way with the thaler or the dollar, the florin or the pound, which are all the same money.

Let us therefore travel these circumvolutions of the ecclesiastical brain, following the noun in pursuit of his adjective. Sílvio calls for Sílvia. And listen; in the distance, it seems that somebody else is sighing, too; it is Sílvia who calls for Sílvio.

They hear each other now, and they seek each other out. And what a difficult, intricate path it is, this brain that is so full with old and new things! There is such a hubbub of ideas in this place, making it hard to hear their calls; let us not lose sight of Sílvio, for there he goes, up and down, slipping and jumping; here, so as not to fall, he grabs hold of a bunch of Latin roots, there he leans upon a psalm, over there he mounts atop a pentameter, and he keeps on walking, carried by an inner force, which he cannot resist.

From time to time, some lady appears to him – another adjective – who offers him her antique or novel charms; but dear God, she is not the same, she is not the one, the one fated *ab aeterno* for this partnership. And Sílvio keeps on walking, in search of the one. Pass by, eyes of every colour, shapes of every caste, hair that has been cut from the head of the Sun or of the Night; die with no echo, sweet ballads sighed on the eternal violin; Sílvio is not asking for just any accidental or anonymous love; he is asking for the right love, named and predestined.

Be not alarmed now, reader, there is no cause for concern; it is merely the canon getting up, going over to the window, and leaning against it, distracting himself from his efforts. There he looks, there he forgets the sermon and all the rest. The parrot on its perch, under the window, repeats its usual words and, in the yard, the peacock puffs up completely in the morning sun; the sun itself, recognising the canon, sends him one of its faithful rays, by way of greeting. And down the ray comes, to stop at the window: "Most illustrious canon, I bring you messages from the sun, my lord and father." And thus all nature seems to clap its hands at the return of that galley-ship of the spirit. He himself is joyful, he casts his eyes around that pure air, allows them to roam, taking their fill of greenery and freshness, to the sounds of a little bird and a piano; then he talks to the parrot, he calls the gardener, he blows his nose, rubs his hands, leans in again. He no longer recalls either Sílvio or Sílvia.

Ah, but Sílvio and Sílvia remember each other still. While the canon is occupied with other things, they continue in their mutual search, as he remains altogether oblivious and unsuspecting. Now, however, their path is dark. We are journeying from consciousness to unconsciousness where the confused elaboration of ideas takes place, where reminiscences sleep or nap. Here abounds life without shape, the seeds and the debris, the fundaments and the sediments; it is the vast attic of the spirit. Here they have landed, in search of each other, calling and sighing. May the reader give me her hand, may the reader clutch me tight with his, and let us slip inside too.

A vast unknown world. Sílvio and Sílvia fight their way through embryos and ruins. Groups of ideas, deduced by means of syllogisms, are lost in the tumult of recollections of childhood and the seminary. Other ideas, pregnant with ideas, drag themselves heavily along, sustained by other ideas that are yet virgin. Things and men fuse; Plato wears the spectacles of a scribe from the ecclesiastical court; mandarins of every class disburse Etruscan and Chilean coins, English books and pale roses; so pale are they that they do not look like the same ones the canon's mother planted when he was a child. Religious and familial memories meet and are commingled. Here are the distant voices from his first mass; and the plantation songs that he used to hear the black women singing, back home; the scraps of faded sensations, a fear here, a pleasure there, and over on that side a distaste at things that appeared each in turn but now lie in this great, dark and impalpable heap.

"Come with me from Lebanon, my bride . . ."

"I conjure you, daughters of Jerusalem . . ."

They can hear each other closer and closer. Now they arrive at the deepest layers of theology, of philosophy, of liturgy, of geography and of history, ancient lessons, modern notions, everything mixed together, dogma and syntax. Here Spinoza's pantheist hand has passed by, secretly; there the scratch from Dr Angelicus; but none of this is Sílvio or Sílvia. And on they go, carried by an inner force, a secret affinity, over every obstacle and across every chasm. Displeasures must come, too. Sombre griefs, which did not linger in the canon's heart, here they are, like moral blemishes, and beside them the yellow or purple reflection, or the whatever it is of the universal pain of others. All of this they cut through, as quick as love and desire.

Are you reeling, dear reader? It is not the world collapsing; it is the canon who has just this moment sat down. He has had his distraction, he returned to his desk, and is now rereading what he wrote, that he might continue; he takes up the nib, wets it, brings it down to the paper, to see which adjective should be attached to the noun.

It is at this exact moment that the eager pair are at their closest to each other. Their voices rise, their enthusiasm rises, the entire Song passes between their fevered lips. Happy phrases, stories from the sacristy, caricatures, witticisms, bits of nonsense, foolish appearances, nothing holds them back, let alone makes them smile. They go, they go, the space is narrowing. Tarry there, part-erased profiles of buffoons that once made the canon laugh, and which he has entirely forgotten; tarry, extinct wrinkles, old riddles, the rules of ombre, and you, too, the seeds of new ideas, the sketching-out of concepts, dust that must have been a pyramid, tarry, collide, hope, despair, for they have nothing to do with you. They love each other and they search for each other.

They search and they find each other. At last, Sílvio has found Sílvia. They espied each other and fell into each other's arms, panting with exhaustion, but redeemed by the reward. They join, they interlink arms, and return pulsating from unconsciousness to consciousness. "Who is this who comes from the desert, leaning upon her beloved?" asks Sílvio, as in the Song; and she, with the same learned lips, replies that it is "the seal of thy heart", and that "love is strong as death itself".

At this, the canon shivers. His face lights up. The nib, full of emotion and respect, completes the noun with the adjective. Sílvia will walk now beside Sílvio, in the sermon that the canon will preach one of these days, and they will go together to the printers, if he collects his writings, which we cannot say.

THE ALIENIST

CHAPTER I

HOW ITAGUAÍ ACQUIRED A LUNATIC ASYLUM

THE CHRONICLERS OF Itaguaí report that the town was home, long ago, to a physician, one Dr Simão Bacamarte, a son of the gentry and the greatest doctor in Brazil, Portugal and the Spains. He had studied at Coimbra and Padua. At the age of thirty-four he had returned to Brazil, His Majesty having been unable to secure his continuing presence in Coimbra, as governor of the university, or in Lisbon, carrying out the business of the monarchy.

"Science," he said to His Majesty, "is my sole employment; Itaguaí is my universe."

With these words, he went off to Itaguaí and surrendered, body and soul, to the study of science. At the age of forty, he married Dona Evarista da Costa e Mascarenhas, a lady of twenty-five, the widow of an itinerant circuit judge, and a woman neither beautiful nor personable. One of his uncles, a mighty hunter of rodents before the Lord, and no less outspoken, wondered at the choice and said as much. Simão Bacamarte explained that D. Evarista combined physiological and anatomical characteristics that were absolutely first-rate, she digested without trouble, was regular in her sleep, had a fine pulse and excellent eyesight; she was thus well suited to giving him children who were robust, healthy and intelligent. If alongside these gifts – the only ones worthy of a scholar's concern – D. Evarista was also ill-favoured, far from regretting this, the doctor thanked God for it, for she thereby ran no risk of displacing scientific interests in her consort's exclusive, narrow and vulgar contemplation.

D. Evarista belied Dr Bacamarte's hopes, giving him no children, neither robust ones nor sickly. The sciences are long-suffering by their very nature; our doctor waited three years, then four, then five. After this time, he carried out an extensive study of the subject, he reread all the Arab writers and others, whom he had brought to Itaguaí, he sent enquiring missives to the Italian and German universities, and ended up counselling his wife to follow an especial diet. This esteemed lady, fed entirely on fine Itaguaí pork, paid no heed to her husband's admonishments; and it is to her resistance – which one might explain, if not appreciate – that we owe the total extinction of the Bacamarte line.

But science has an undeniable gift for curing all hurts; our doctor immersed himself entirely in the study and practice of medicine. It was then that one of its smaller niches caught his particular attention – that of psychology, the examination of maladies of the brain. The colony, and indeed the kingdom, had not one single authority on such matters, which were poorly explored if they were explored at all. Simão Bacamarte understood that Lusitanian science, and the science found in Brazil particularly, might cover itself in "laurels everlasting" – this was the phrase he himself used, though only in a rapture of domestic privacy; outwardly he was modest, as is befitting of learned men.

"The health of the soul," he proclaimed, "is the doctor's worthiest occupation."

"The true doctor's," added Crispim Soares, the town apothecary, who was one of his friends and dining companions.

The Itaguaí Town Council, among other sins of which the chroniclers accuse it, sinned in its failure to tend to the insane. That was how every raging mad person came to be locked away in a little room, in his own house, thereby obscured rather than cured, until death came to cheat him of the favours of life; while the docile ones were left to wander freely about the streets. Simão Bacamarte sought from the outset to reform this bad habit; he requested the Council's permission to construct a building in which he might corral and treat all the mad people of Itaguaí and of the other towns and cities, in exchange for a stipend, which the Council would give him whenever the sick person's family was unable to pay it. The proposal excited the whole town's curiosity, and met with great resistance, it being beyond question that it is not easy to disentangle oneself from foolish habits, or even bad ones. The idea of putting all the mad people in the same house, living communally, seemed itself a symptom of lunacy, and there were those who made such insinuations to the doctor's own wife.

"Look, Dona Evarista," said Father Lopes, the local vicar, "you should see to it that your husband takes a trip to Rio de Janeiro. His habit of being always at his studies, always, this sort of behaviour is not good, it can turn a man's reason."

D. Evarista was appalled, and she went to her husband and said that she "had longings", one in particular, to travel to Rio de Janeiro and eat everything he felt appropriate to a certain end. But the great man, with the rare shrewdness that distinguished him, grasped his wife's intentions and retorted with a smile that she ought not to be afraid. He went thence to the Council chamber, where the councillors were debating his proposal, and he defended it with such eloquence that the majority resolved to authorise his request, voting simultaneously for a tax that would subsidise the treatment, housing and upkeep of the poor lunatics. The object of the tax could not be easily found; everything in Itaguaí had a tax already. After much study, they resolved to license the use of two plumes on the undertakers' horses. Anybody who wished to use a plume on the horses of a carriage-hearse would pay the Council two tostões, this small sum being repeated as many times as there were hours that passed between the demise and the final graveside blessing. The clerk got tangled up in the arithmetical calculations of the possible income from the new levy; and one of the councilmen, who was sceptical about the doctor's enterprise, asked that the clerk be relieved of this useless job.

"The calculations are not precise," he said, "because Dr Bacamarte is not getting anything done.

And who ever imagined putting all the lunatics together into the same house?"

The worthy legislator was incorrect; the doctor got everything done. Once he had obtained the permit, he began at once to build the house. It was on Rua Nova, then the loveliest street in Itaguaí, it had fifty windows on each side, a central courtyard, and countless cubicles for the residents. And, great Arabist that he was, he discovered in the Quran that Mohammed had declared lunatics worthy of reverence, owing to the belief that Allah had taken away their reason that they might not sin. He thought this idea beautiful and profound, and had it engraved on the frontispiece of the house; but being fearful of upsetting the vicar, and indirectly the bishop, he attributed the thought to Benedict VIII, earning for himself by this fraud, which was indeed a pious one, a lecture from Father Lopes, over lunch, on that eminent pontiff's life.

The Casa Verde was the name given to the asylum, in reference to the colour of the windows, which were green for the first time in Itaguaí. The establishment was opened with the greatest pomp; from all the nearby towns and settlements, and even from distant ones, and the city of Rio de Janeiro itself, people flocked to attend the commemorations, which lasted seven days. Many mad people had been assembled already; and relatives had the opportunity to witness the fatherly care and Christian charity with which they would be treated. D. Evarista, immensely pleased at her husband's glory, had dressed lavishly, bedecking herself in jewels, flowers and silks. She was a true queen on those memorable days; nobody failed to call on her two or three times, despite the modest domestic customs of that century, and they did not merely court her but sang her praises; seeing as – and this fact is a real credit to the society of the time – seeing as they saw in her the happy wife of a lofty spirit, of a distinguished gentleman, and if they did feel any envy towards her, it was the holy and noble envy of an admirer. When the seven days had come to an end, the public festivities drew to a close; Itaguaí had an insane asylum at last.

CHAPTER II
FLOODS OF LUNATICS

THREE DAYS LATER, in a burst of private eloquence with the apothecary Crispim Soares, the alienist uncovered the very mystery of his heart.

"Charity, Senhor Soares, certainly does come into my procedures, but it is added as the seasoning, as the salt of things, this being how I interpret Saint Paul's words to the Corinthians: 'If I know all that might be known, but have not charity, then am I nothing.' The crux of this work of mine at the Casa Verde is the in-depth study of madness, its varying degrees, the classifying of its cases; in short, discovering the cause of the phenomenon and its universal remedy. This is the mystery of my heart. I believe I might thereby do humanity some service."

"Some excellent service," the apothecary corrected him.

"Without this asylum," the alienist continued, "I could not do much; however, it gives me much greater scope for my studies."

"Much greater," the other man added.

And they were right. From all the neighbouring towns and villages, crazy people flowed in to the Casa Verde. They were raging, they were docile, they were monomaniacal, they were the whole family of the disinherited of the mind. In four months, the Casa Verde was a village. Those first cubicles were insufficient; the addition of a gallery of a further thirty-seven was commissioned. Father Lopes confessed he had never imagined that so many lunatics might exist in the world, let alone how inexplicable some of these cases might be. One of them, for example, a coarse peasant lad, who each day, after lunch, would give an academic lecture, adorned with tropes, with antitheses, with apostrophes, with ornaments of Greek and Latin, and more flourishes from Cicero, Apuleius and Tertulian. The vicar could not believe it. How could it be?! A lad he had seen, three months earlier, playing shuttlecock on the street!

"Indeed so," replied the alienist, "but the truth is just what Your Reverence is seeing. An everyday occurrence."

"If you ask me," retorted the priest, "the only possible explanation is to be found in the muddle of tongues from the Tower of Babel, as the Scriptures tell us; most likely, since languages were confused in ancient times, it is easy to interchange them now, provided that one's reason is not working . . ."

"That might indeed be so, a divine explanation for the phenomenon," agreed the alienist, after a moment's reflection, "but it is not impossible that there should be some other reason that is human, and purely scientific, and that is what I seek to—"

"Perhaps so, and I am most eager to learn. Truly!"

Those who were mad for love numbered three or four, but only two were especially surprising in the strangeness of their delirium. The first, one Falcão, a youth of twenty-five, supposed himself the morning star, he would open his arms and stretch out his legs, to give them something of the appearance of beams, and spent hours on end in this way asking whether the sun had come out in order that he might withdraw. The other would walk, constantly, round and round and round the halls or the courtyard, and up and down the corridors, in search of the end of the world. He was a wretched man, whose wife had left him to follow some popinjay. No sooner had he learned of her flight than he armed himself with a small pistol, and set out in their pursuit; he found them two hours later, beside a lagoon, and killed them both with the greatest extremes of cruelty.

Jealousy was satisfied, but the avenged man had turned mad. Then began that great eagerness of going to the end of the world in search of the fugitives.

Delusions of grandeur had some notable exemplars. The most notable of all was one poor devil, the son of a slop-seller, who would recount to the walls (for he never looked at another soul) his entire genealogy, which was as follows:

"God begat an egg, the egg begat the sword, the sword begat David, David begat purple, purple begat the duke, the duke begat the marquis, the marquis begat the count, who is me."

He would slap his forehead, click his fingers, and repeat five or six times in a row:

"God begat an egg, the egg etc."

Another patient of the same species was a clerk who claimed to be the king's butler; another was a drover from Minas, whose obsession was handing out herds of cattle to everyone, he would give three hundred head to one person, six hundred to another, twelve hundred to the next, and it was never-ending. I shall not speak of the cases of religious monomania; I will refer only to one fellow who, calling himself João of God, said that he was now the God João, and promised the kingdom of heaven to whosoever adored him, and the pains of hell to the rest; and after him, the young graduate Garcia, who said nothing, for he imagined that on the day when he uttered one single word, all the stars would become detached from the sky and scorch the earth; such was the power that God had bestowed upon him.

This he wrote on the piece of paper that the alienist had allowed him, less out of charity than scientific interest.

Yet the alienist's patience was even more remarkable than all the insanities residing in the Casa Verde; no less than astonishing. Simão Bacamarte began by organising some administrative personnel; and having accepted this idea from the apothecary Crispim Soares, he also accepted two nephews from him, whom he tasked with carrying out the instructions that he gave them, approved by the Council, for distributing the clothes and food, as well as keeping the books, etc. It was his best course of action, that he might dedicate himself entirely to his office. "The Casa Verde," he said to the vicar, "is now a kind of world, in which there is a temporal government and a spiritual government." And Father Lopes laughed at this pious joke, and added, aiming only to contribute a witticism of his own: "That's enough, that's enough, or I shall have to report you to the Pope."

Once unburdened of the administrative tasks, the alienist proceeded to carry out a vast classification of his patients. He divided them first into two principal categories: the raging and the docile; then he moved on to sub-classes, monomanias, deliria, miscellaneous delusions. This completed, he set about a protracted and uninterrupted study; he analysed the habits of each mad person, the timing of their fits, their dislikes, their likes, their words, their gestures, their habits; he inquired after the patients' lives, their professions, customs, the circumstances of the illness's first manifestation, any accidents suffered in childhood and youth, illnesses of other kinds, family precedents, an investigation, in short, such as not even the cleverest comptroller would undertake. And each day he noted down some new observation, some interesting discovery, some extraordinary phenomenon. At the same time, he was studying the best diet, the medicinal substances, the curative means and the palliative means, not only those that came from his beloved Arabs, but those he discovered for himself, by dint of shrewdness and patience. And all this work took the best part of his time. He barely slept and he barely ate; and even when eating, it was as if he was still at work, for he was now interrogating some ancient text, now contemplating some question, and he would frequently go from one end of dinner to the other without directing a single word to D. Evarista.

CHAPTER III
GOD KNOWS WHAT HE IS DOING!

THIS ESTEEMED LADY, after two months, thought herself the most wretched of women; she fell into a deep melancholy, she turned yellow, thin, eating little and sighing wherever she went. She dared not make any complaint or reproach, for she respected him as her husband and her lord, but she suffered silently, and withered visibly away. One day, at dinner, when her husband asked what ailed her, she replied sadly that it was nothing; then she dared a little further and was about to say that she felt as much a widow as she had before. And she added:

"Who would ever have thought that half a dozen lunatics . . ."

She did not complete her sentence; she finally raised her eyes to the ceiling – those eyes that were her most engaging feature: black, large eyes, bathed in a humid light, like those of the dawn. As for the action, it was the same that she had employed on the day Simão Bacamarte requested her hand in marriage. The town chronicles do not report whether D. Evarista wielded that weapon with the perverse intention of decapitating science once and for all, or, at least, chopping off its hands; but the conjecture is a plausible one. In any case, the alienist ascribed no other intention to her. And the great man was not irritated, not even slightly vexed. The metal of his eyes continued to be the same metal, hard, smooth, eternal, and not the least crease broke the surface of that forehead as becalmed as the waters of the bay at Botafogo. Perhaps a smile unclenched his lips, between which filtered these words as smooth as the ointments from the Song of Songs:

"I give my consent for you to take a trip to Rio de Janeiro."

D. Evarista felt the floor disappear beneath her feet. Never ever had she seen Rio de Janeiro, which, while it was not even a shadow of what it is today, was nonetheless somewhat more than Itaguaí. Seeing Rio de Janeiro, for her, was equivalent to the dream of the Hebrew slave. Now, especially, that her husband had settled for good into that village in the interior, now she had lost any remaining hope of breathing the airs of our fine city; and it was just now that he should invite her to make the dreams of her childhood and youth a reality. D. Evarista was unable to disguise her delight at such a proposal. Simão Bacamarte took her hand and smiled – a smile that was somewhat philosophical, as well as conjugal, which seemed a translation of this thought:

"There is no sure remedy for the pains of the soul; this lady is withering away, because she believes I do not love her; I shall give her Rio de Janeiro, and she will be consoled." And because he was a scholarly man, he took a note of this observation.

Another dart pierced D. Evarista's breast. She restrained herself, however, and merely said to her husband that, if he did not go, she would not go either, because there was no question of her venturing onto the highways alone.

"You will go with your aunt," replied the alienist.

We should note that D. Evarista had thought of this herself; but she had not wanted to ask for it nor to imply it, first because it would mean imposing significant costs on her husband, second because it was best, more methodical and rational, for the proposal to come from him.

"Oh, but that would mean spending so very much money!" sighed D. Evarista without conviction.

"What does that matter? We have earned a great deal," said her husband. "Only yesterday the clerk presented the accounts to me. Would you care to see?"

And he led her to the books. D. Evarista was amazed. It was a whole Milky Way of figures. And then he led her to the chests, where the money was.

Lord! There were piles of gold, thousands upon thousands of cruzados, doubloons upon doubloons; it was sheer opulence.

While she ate up the gold with her dark eyes, the alienist stared at her, murmuring in her ear the most mischievous of allusions:

"Who would ever have thought that half a dozen lunatics . . ."

D. Evarista understood, smiled and replied, altogether resigned:

"God knows what he is doing!"

Three months later the journey was all set to be realised. D. Evarista, her aunt, the apothecary's wife, one of their nephews, a priest whom the alienist had met in Lisbon, and who happened to find himself in Itaguaí, five or six pages, four maids, such was the retinue that the town's population saw departing one morning in the month of May. The farewells were sad for everybody except for the alienist. Although D. Evarista's tears were abundant and sincere, they never managed to shake him. A man of science, and science alone, was never shocked by anything outside of science; and if something did trouble him on that occasion, if he did allow himself to scan the crowd with a concerned and policeman-like look, it was nothing more than the idea that some deranged person might find himself mixed up there among the people of reason.

"Farewell!" the ladies and the apothecary sobbed at last.

And the retinue set off. As Crispim Soares returned home, his eyes were set between the two ears of the roan animal on which he rode; Simão Bacamarte cast his own eyes out towards the horizon before him, leaving the responsibility for their return to his horse. A lively picture of the genius and the common man! One stares at the present, with all its tears and absences, the other probes the future with all its dawns.

CHAPTER IV
A NEW THEORY

W HILST D. EVARISTA was on her tearful way to Rio de Janeiro, Simão Bacamarte was fully occupied studying an idea that was quite bold and new, fit to expand the very foundations of psychology. All the time he had to spare from the Casa Verde was not enough for walking the streets, or from house to house, talking to people, on thirty thousand subjects, and punctuating his talking with a look that struck fear into even the most heroic of hearts.

One morning – three weeks had gone by – as Crispim Soares was busy mixing a remedy, he received word that the alienist had called for him.

"On an important matter, from what he told me," added the bearer of the message.

Crispim paled. What important matter could it be, if not some news lately arrived from the retinue, and especially some news of his wife? For we ought to leave this matter quite clear, given that the chroniclers of the town insisted upon it: Crispim loved his wife, and in thirty years they had not been parted a single day. This would explain his monologues now, which his servants heard from him often – "Well then, serves you right, who told you to agree to Cesária's trip, eh? Sycophant, vile sycophant! Just to flatter Dr Bacamarte! Well, now you can put up with it; go on, just put up with it, pathetic flunkey, weakling, loathsome wretch. You'll say amen to anything, won't you? Well, there's your reward, peasant!" And many other harsh names that a man ought not to address to another, let alone to himself. From there to imagining the effect of the alienist's message is no distance at all. He received it with such speed that he dropped the drugs and flew over to the Casa Verde.

Simão Bacamarte received him with the joy befitting a learned man, a joy that was buttoned up to the neck with circumspection.

"I'm so glad," he said.

"News from our people?" asked the apothecary, his voice aquiver.

The alienist gave a grand gesture, and replied:

"Oh, a loftier matter than that, concerning a scientific experiment. I say experiment, for I dare not confidently assert my idea right away; science is nothing, Senhor Soares, but a constant investigation. It is, then, an experiment, but an experiment that will alter the face of the earth. Madness, the object of my studies, has hitherto been an island lost in the ocean of reason; I am beginning to suspect it is rather a continent."

He said this, then fell silent, contemplating the apothecary's amazement. Then he explained his idea at length. As he conceived it, insanity covered a vast spread of brains, and he developed this idea with a great abundance of reasoned arguments, of texts, of examples. The examples he had found in history and in Itaguaí, but, rare spirit that he was, he recognised the danger of citing all his cases from Itaguaí and took refuge in history. Thus, he named certain celebrated personages, Socrates, who had a demon familiar, Pascal, who sensed an abyss always to his left, Mohammed, Caracalla, Domitian, Caligula, etc., a string of cases and people, with some loathsome creatures and ridiculous ones mixed in. And since the apothecary marvelled at such variety, the alienist told him it was all the same, and even added, sententiously:

"Ferocity, Senhor Soares, is merely the grotesque taken seriously."

"Delightful, quite delightful!" exclaimed Crispim Soares, raising his hands towards the heavens.

As for the idea of enlarging the territory of madness, the apothecary thought it excessive; but modesty, which was the principal ornament of his spirit, would not allow him to confess anything but the noblest enthusiasm; he declared it to be sublime and true, and added that it was "worth the rattle". This expression has no equivalent in the modern style. In those days, Itaguaí, like the other towns, villages and settlements in the colony, had no press, so there were two ways of disseminating a piece of news: either by means of handwritten posters pinned to the door of the Council chamber and of the mother church; or by means of a rattle. This is what that second practice entailed. A man would be contracted, for one day or more, to walk the streets with a rattle in his hand. From time to time he would sound the rattle, people would gather about him, and he would pronounce whatever he had been charged with – a remedy for agues, some arable lands, a sonnet, an ecclesiastical donation, the worst slanderer in town, most beautiful speech of the year, etc. The system had its inconveniences as regarded the public peace; but it was retained for the great disseminating vigour that it possessed. For example, one of the councilmen – the very one who had been most opposed to the creation of the Casa Verde – enjoyed the reputation of being a peerless teacher of snakes and monkeys, while actually he had never tamed even one of these beasts; but he did take

"Honestly, he did not deserve that . . . And on top of everything! After everything he had done . . ."

Costa was one of Itaguaí's most esteemed citizens. He had inherited four hundred thousand cruzados in good coin of His Majesty Dom João V, the income from which money was enough, according to his uncle's will, to live "until the end of the world". No sooner had he collected his inheritance than he set about dividing it up into loans, without interest, a thousand cruzados to one person, two thousand to another, three hundred to that one, eight hundred to this, up to the point where, five years on, he had nothing left. If total poverty had come upon him all of a sudden, Itaguaí's astonishment would have been enormous; but it came slowly; he passed from opulence to abundance, from abundance to sufficiency, from sufficiency to poverty, from poverty to wretchedness, gradually. After those five years, people who had once bowed low with doffed hats, as soon as he appeared at the end of the road, now clapped him on the shoulder most familiarly, they tweaked his nose, they insulted him. And Costa always amiable, always cheerful. He did not even let on that those who were the least courteous towards him were precisely those who had debts outstanding; on the contrary, he seemed to welcome them with the greater pleasure, and the noblest resignation. One day, when one of these incurable debtors flung a coarse jibe at him, and he laughed at it, a certain cynic observed, rather spitefully: "You only tolerate this fellow to see whether he might pay you." Costa did not pause for a minute, he went to the debtor and forgave him his debt. "No wonder," replied the other man. "Costa let go of a star, which is in the sky." Costa was shrewd, and he understood that the man was denying any merit in his act, attributing to him the intention of rejecting what would not be put into his pocket anyway. But he was a man of self-respect, too, and inventive; two hours later, he found a way of proving that such a slur did not fit him: he took some doubloons and sent them on loan to the debtor.

"I hope now that . . ." he thought, without completing the sentence.

This last act of Costa's persuaded believers and disbelievers alike; no one ever cast doubt upon the gallant feelings of that worthy citizen again. The shyest of the needy went out onto the street, they came to knock on his door, with their worn old shoes, with their patched cloaks. A little worm, however, still gnawed at Costa's soul: it was that cynic's opinion. But even this ended; three months later this same man came to ask him for a hundred and twenty cruzados on a promise that it would be repaid two days later; this was all that remained of the great inheritance, but it was also a noble redress: Costa loaned the money right away, right away and without any interest. Unfortunately he did not have time to get paid; five months later he was taken into the Casa Verde.

Just imagine the great dismay in Itaguaí when they learned of the affair. There was no other topic of conversation; some said that Costa had lost his mind at lunch, others that it was in the small hours; and people told stories about his attacks, which were raging, dark, terrible – or docile, and even amusing, depending on the version. Many people rushed to the Casa Verde, where they found Costa, quite calm, somewhat surprised, talking with great clarity, and asking the reason for his having been brought to that place. Some went to talk to the alienist. Bacamarte approved of these feelings of esteem and compassion, but added that science was science, and he could not leave a crazy person out on the street. The last to intercede on his behalf (for after what I am about to relate, nobody else dared to seek the terrible doctor out) was an unfortunate woman, Costa's cousin. The alienist told her in confidence that the worthy man did not have his mental faculties in perfect equilibrium, judging by the way he had squandered those riches which . . .

"Oh no, not that!" the good woman interrupted energetically. "If he spent his inheritance so quickly, that is not his fault."

"It is not?"

"No, senhor. I can tell you how the matter occurred. My late uncle was not a bad man; but when he was in a rage he was quite capable of not doffing his cap even to the Blessed Host. Well, one day, shortly before his death, he discovered that a slave had stolen an ox; imagine the state this put him in. His face was a red-pepper; his entire body trembled, his mouth frothed; I remember it as if it was today. Then an ugly, hairy man in his shirtsleeves came to him and asked for water. My uncle (may God speak kindly to his soul!) replied that he should go drink at the river or go to hell. The man looked at him, opened his palm as if by way of a threat, and spoke this curse: 'All your money shall not last more than seven year and a day, as surely as this is the Seal of Solomon!' And he showed him the Seal of Solomon tattooed on his arm. And that, senhor, was it; this was the damned man's curse."

Bacamarte had stabbed the poor lady with a pair of eyes as sharp as daggers. When she had finished, he held out his hand politely, as if to the viceroy's wife

139

herself, and invited her to come speak to her cousin. The poor wretch believed him; he took her to the Casa Verde and shut her up in the delusional ward.

The news of this treachery by the eminent Bacamarte struck terror into the souls of the populace. Nobody wanted to believe that, with no good reason, with no especial enmity, the alienist had locked up in the Casa Verde a woman of perfectly judicious mind, who had committed no other crime than interceding on behalf of a person in misfortune. The affair was chattered about on street corners, in barbershops; an entire novel was constructed, with some amorous attentions that the alienist had once directed at Costa's cousin, and Costa's outrage and the cousin's contempt. Hence this revenge. It was quite clear. Yet the alienist's austerity, his life of study, seemed to belie such a hypothesis. All fiction! All this was naturally the crook's façade. And one of the more credulous people would even murmur that he knew of other things, he would not say them, not being absolutely sure, but he knew them, he could almost swear.

"But you, you're so close to him, could you not tell us what is happening, what has happened, what reason . . ."

Crispim Soares was melting completely. All this questioning from people who were concerned and

curious, from astonished friends, was a public conse-
cration to him. There was no doubting it; the whole
town did know after all that the alienist's closest friend
was him, Crispim, the apothecary, the great man's
collaborator in great things; hence the flurry of visits
to the dispensary. All this was expressed by the apothecary's jocund expression and discreet laughter, his
laughter and his silence, for he made no reply; one,
two, three monosyllables, at most, disconnected, curt,
cloaked in his faithful, constant little smile, filled with
scientific mysteries, which he could not, without
dishonour or danger, reveal to any human soul.

"Something is afoot," thought the more suspicious
of his visitors.

One of these men merely thought it, shrugged
and went off. He had personal business to attend to.
He had just built a lavish new house. The house alone
was enough to attract anybody's notice; but there was
more: the furniture, which he had ordered from
Hungary and Holland, so he said, and which could
be seen from outside, because the windows were
forever open – and the garden, which was a masterpiece of art and taste. This man, who had made his
fortune in the manufacture of saddles, had always
dreamed of a magnificent house, an ostentatious
garden, rare furniture. He had not left the saddle

business, but was finding some respite from it, in his contemplation of the new house, the first in Itaguaí, grander even than the Casa Verde, nobler than the Council building itself. Among the distinguished people in this little town, there was some weeping and grinding of teeth, when they thought of, or spoke of, or praised the house of the saddler – a simple saddler, for heaven's sake!

"He's out there gawking," the passers-by would say, in the morning.

In the morning, it was indeed Mateus's custom to lounge in the middle of the garden, his eyes on the house, besotted, for a long hour, until somebody came to call him in for lunch. The neighbours, while they greeted him with a certain respect, laughed behind his back, greatly amused. One of them even said that Mateus would save much more money, and would be immensely rich, if he made the saddles for himself; a quip that was incomprehensible but which sent them into billowing laughter.

"And there's Mateus now, getting himself looked at," they would say in the afternoon.

The reason for this other saying was that, in the afternoon, when families were taking a stroll (they had their dinner early), Mateus was in the habit of positioning himself at the window, right in the centre, conspicuous, against a dark background, all dressed in white, in a lordly posture, and he would spend two or three hours there until night had completely fallen. One might believe that Mateus's intention was to be admired and envied, though he had not confessed it to anyone, not even to the apothecary nor to Father Lopes, his great friends. And the apothecary's protestation was exactly this, when the alienist told him that the saddler might be suffering from a love for stones, a mania that he, Bacamarte, had discovered and had been studying for some time. That whole business of gazing at the house . . .

"Oh no, senhor," replied Crispim Soares animatedly.

"No?"

"You must forgive me, but perhaps you are unaware that he spends his mornings examining the work, not admiring it; in the afternoons, it is others who admire the work and him." And he described the saddler's custom, every afternoon, from early until nightfall.

A scientific ecstasy lit up Simão Bacamarte's eyes. Either he did not know all of the saddler's habits, or all he wanted, in questioning Crispim, was to confirm some uncertain report or vague suspicion. He was satisfied with the explanation; but since his joys were those befitting a learned man, which were concentrated ones, the apothecary saw nothing that led him to suspect any sinister intent. On the contrary, it was afternoon now, and the alienist offered him his arm that they might take a stroll. Oh Lord! This was the first time Simão Bacamarte had bestowed such an honour on his dear friend; Crispim was trembling, flustered, he said yes, he was all ready to go. Two or three other people came in, and Crispim told them mentally to go to the devil; not only were they delaying their walk, but Bacamarte might choose one of them to accompany him, and then the apothecary would be dispensed with entirely. Such impatience! Such anxiety! At last, they walked out. The alienist led them towards the saddler's house, saw him at the window, walked five, six times past the house, slowly, stopping, examining the man's postures, the expression on his face. Poor Mateus, no sooner had he noticed that he was the object of curiosity or admiration by Itaguaí's preeminent personage than he intensified his expression, accentuated his poses . . . So sad! So sad! He was just condemning himself; the following day, he was taken into the Casa Verde.

"The Casa Verde is a private prison," said one doctor who had no clinic of his own.

Never did an opinion catch on and tear through the population so fast. A private prison: it was repeated from north to south, from the east of Itaguaí to the consort, in a gesture that can only be defined as resembling a mixture of jaguar and turtle-dove. Not so the distinguished Bacamarte; cold as a diagnosis, not disengaging his scientific rigidity for a moment, he held out his arms to the lady who fell into them and fainted. It did not last; two minutes later, D. Evarista was greeted by her friends and the convoy set off.

D. Evarista was the hope of Itaguaí; they counted on her to moderate the scourge of the Casa Verde. Hence all the public acclamation, the vast crowd thronging the streets, the pennants, the flowers and damasks in the windows. Her arm resting on that of Father Lopes – for the distinguished Bacamarte had entrusted his wife to the vicar, and was walking beside them, lost in thought – D. Evarista turned her head this way and that, edgy, curious, brazen. The vicar enquired after Rio de Janeiro, which he had not seen since the previous vice-regency; and D. Evarista responded, enthusiastically, that it was the most beautiful thing that could possibly exist in all the world. The Passeio Público was finished, a paradise where she had been many times, and the Rua das Belas Noites, the Marrecas Fountain . . . Oh, the Marrecas Fountain! They really were actual Marreca ducks – made of metal and spouting water from their beaks. The most elegant thing you can imagine! The vicar

said yes, Rio de Janeiro must be so much more beautiful now. Seeing as it was beautiful even back in the
day! And no wonder, bigger than Itaguaí, and, what
was more, the seat of government . . . Yet one could
not say that Itaguaí was ugly; it had beautiful houses,
Mateus's house, the Casa Verde . . .

"On the subject of the Casa Verde," said Father
Lopes, slipping artfully onto the matter of the day, "I
believe, senhora, you will find it rather full of
people."

"Is that so?"

"Yes. Mateus is there . . ."

"The saddler?"

"The saddler; Costa is there, and Costa's cousin,
and so-and-so, and what's-his-name, and . . ."

"So many insane people?"

"Or almost insane," the priest demurred.

"And so . . .?"

The vicar turned down the corners of his mouth,
like somebody who knows nothing or does not want to
say everything; a vague reply, which could never be
repeated to another person owing to the lack of any
actual text. D. Evarista found it truly extraordinary
that all those people had lost their wits; one or other of
them, certainly; but all? Yet nor was it easy to doubt;
her husband was a learned man, he would never take

anyone into the Casa Verde without clear proof of madness.

"Of course . . . of course . . ." the vicar continued to punctuate her words.

Three hours later, some fifty guests sat down around Simão Bacamarte's table; it was the welcome dinner. D. Evarista was the compulsory subject of the toasts, speeches, all manner of verses, metaphors, exaggerations, apologues. She was the wife of the new Hippocrates, the muse of science, angel, divine, dawn, charity, life, consolation; in her eyes were two stars, according to Crispim Soares's modest version, and two suns, in the conceit of one councilman. The alienist listened to these things rather bored, but without any visible impatience. At most he would whisper into his wife's ear that rhetoric does indeed allow for such meaningless boldness. D. Evarista did try to join her husband in this opinion; but even if she discounted three-quarters of the fawning, much still remained with which to puff up her soul. One of the speakers, for example, Martim Brito, a lad of twenty-five, a consummate fop, a lover of romances and adventures, delivered a speech in which the birth of D. Evarista was explained by the most singular of feats. "God," he said, "after bestowing upon the universe man and woman, that diamond and pearl of the divine crown,"

– and the speaker dragged this little phrase trium-
phantly from one end of the table to the other – "God
wished to vanquish God, and He created Dona
Evarista."

D. Evarista lowered her eyes with exemplary
modesty. Two ladies, who were finding this man's
courtliness excessive and insolent, threw a questioning glance at the eyes of their host; and in truth, the
alienist's expression did seem to them to be clouded
over with suspicions, with threats and, most likely,
with blood. The boldness was very great, the two
ladies thought. And both asked God to take any
tragic episode away – or to defer it, at least to the
following day. Yes, postpone it. One of them, the
more pious of the two, even admitted, to herself, that
D. Evarista did not deserve any distrust, so far was
she from being attractive or beautiful. Quite insipid.
But the truth was, if everyone had the same taste,
what would become of yellow? This idea made her
tremble once again, though less this time; less,
because the alienist was now smiling at Martim Brito
and, when everyone had got up, he went over to him
and said something about his speech. He didn't deny
that it had been a dazzling improvisation, full of
magnificent strokes. Had the idea regarding D.
Evarista's birth really been his or had he found it in

some author who . . .? Oh no, senhor; it was really his; he had found it on that very occasion and felt it suitable for an oratorical rapture. Besides, his ideas were more daring than tender or jocular. He inclined towards the epic. Once, for example, he had composed an ode to the fall of the Marquis of Pombal, in which he said that the minister was "the fierce dragon of Nothing", crushed by the "vengeful claws of Everything"; and likewise others more or less out of the ordinary; he liked ideas that were sublime and rare, images great and noble . . .

"Poor boy!" thought the alienist. And he continued, to himself: "This is a case of brain damage; not too serious a phenomenon, but one worthy of study . . ."

D. Evarista was dumbfounded to learn, three days later, that Martim Brito had been accommodated in the Casa Verde. A boy with such lovely ideas! The two ladies attributed the act to jealousy on the alienist's part. There was no other explanation; the boy's declaration had indeed been too bold.

Jealousy? But how then to explain the fact that, immediately after this, José Borges do Couto Leme, a person of great esteem, was taken in, and Chico das Cambraias, a most notable reveller, and the clerk Fabrício and others besides? The terror was heightened. People no longer knew who was sane, and who was mad. The women of the town, when their husbands went out, would have a lamp lit to Our Lady; and it was hardly the case that every husband was himself valiant, for some did not leave the house at all without one or two bodyguards. Genuine terror. Anybody who could, moved away. One of these fugitives was caught a couple of hundred paces from the town. He was a young man of thirty, pleasant, talkative, well-mannered, so well-mannered that he never greeted another person without bowing low, hat doffed; on the street he had been known to run a distance of thirty or forty yards to shake the hand of a serious man, a lady, sometimes a young boy, as had happened with the itinerant judge's son. Courtesy was his vocation. Besides, he owed his good relations with society not only to his personal gifts, which were exceptional, but also to the noble tenacity that would never falter even when faced with one, two, four, six rebuffs, hostile expressions, etc. What happened was, once he was in a house, he would never leave it again, and nor would those who lived there have him do so, so charming was Gil Bernardes. So Gil Bernardes, though he knew himself to be well-regarded, was afraid when he learned one day that the alienist had his eye on him; early the next morning, he fled the

And nobody answered him; everyone kept repeating that he was a perfectly sane man. The same lawsuit that he was bringing against the barber, about some land in the town, was born of the obscurity of a permit and not of greed or hatred. A fine character, that Coelho. His only detractors were a few fellows who, claiming to be reticent, or professing to be in a hurry, no sooner did they spy him from afar than they turned corners, went into shops, etc. The truth was, he loved making fine conversation, unhurried chats that he savoured in long draughts, and thus it was that he was never alone, preferring those people who knew how to say two words, though not disdaining the others. Father Lopes, who had studied Dante, and was an enemy of Coelho's, never once saw him turn his back on someone without reciting and amending this passage:

> *La bocca sollevò dal fiero pasto*
> *Quel "seccatore" . . .*

but some already knew of the priest's hatred, and others thought this was a prayer in Latin.

CHAPTER VI
THE REVOLT

AROUND THIRTY PEOPLE joined forces with the barber; they drafted a petition and presented it to the Town Council.

The Council refused to accept it, declaring that the Casa Verde was a public institution, and that science could not be amended by some administrative vote, let alone by a bit of unrest on the street.

"You should all return to work," the Council president concluded, "that is our advice."

The agitators were tremendously angry. The barber declared that they would go and raise the flag of rebellion and destroy the Casa Verde; that Itaguaí could not go on serving as a cadaver for the studies and experiments of a despot; that many estimable people, and some distinguished ones, and others who were humble but yet worthy of consideration, were languishing in the Casa Verde cells; that the alienist's scientific despotism was getting mixed up with the spirit of greed, given that the crazy people, or those alleged to be so, were not being treated for free: their families, and in their absence, the Council, were paying the alienist . . .

"That is false!" the president interrupted him.

"False?"

"About three weeks ago, we received an official letter from the distinguished doctor in which he states that, while seeking to carry out experiments of great psychological value, he is renouncing the stipend voted for by the Council, as well as receiving nothing from the sick people's families."

The news of such an act, so noble, so pure, did curb the rebels' spirits somewhat. The alienist might certainly be mistaken, but he had no interest beyond science spurring him on; and if they meant to demonstrate his mistake, they would need more than riots and outcry. Thus spoke the president, to the applause of the whole Council. The barber, after a few moments' reflection, declared that a public mandate had been invested in him and he would not restore peace to Itaguaí until he beheld the Casa Verde razed to the ground – that *Bastille of human reason* – an expression he'd heard from a local poet and which he repeated most emphatically. He said this, and upon a certain signal everybody left with him.

Just imagine the councilmen's position; it was essential that they prevent mass gatherings, revolt, fighting, bloodshed. To make matters worse, one of the councilmen, who had supported the president, now hearing the name given by the barber to the Casa

Verde – "Bastille of human reason" – thought it so elegant that he changed his mind. He said he understood the good sense of introducing some measure that would reduce the Casa Verde; and because the president, annoyed, showed his surprise in energetic terms, the councilman reflected thus:

"I have no idea about science; but if so many people whom we believe to be of sound mind are locked away as lunatics, who is to say that it is not the mad-doctor himself who is mad?"

Sebastião Freitas, this dissenting councilman, had the gift of the gab and he spoke for some while longer, prudently but firmly. His colleagues were astonished; the president asked that he, at least, set an example of order and respect for the law, that he not share his ideas in public, so as not to unite the revolt, which for now was just a whirlwind of disparate individuals. This figure of speech corrected the effect of the previous one somewhat: Sebastião Freitas promised to suspend any action, only reserving for himself the right to request by legal means the reduction in the Casa Verde. And he went on repeating to himself, enchanted: "Bastille of human reason!"

However, the disorder on the streets was growing. There were no longer thirty but three hundred people accompanying the barber, whose common nickname ought to be mentioned here, because it gave its name to the rebellion; they called him Canjica, after the kind of porridge – and the movement became famous as the Porridge Rebellion. Action might be limited, given that many people, either through fear or through habits of upbringing, did not come out onto the streets; but the sentiment was unanimous, or almost unanimous, and the three hundred who walked to the Casa Verde – taking into consideration the difference between Paris and Itaguaí – could indeed be compared to those who stormed the Bastille.

D. Evarista received news of the rebellion before it arrived; she learned of it from one of her slave boys. She was on this occasion trying out a silk dress – one of the thirty-seven she had brought from Rio de Janeiro – and she did not want to believe it.

"There must surely be some revellers out," she said, altering the position of a pin. "Benedita, tell me if this hem looks right."

"Oh yes, mistress," replied the slave woman who was squatting on the floor, "it is good. Mistress turn a little. Like that. Is very good."

"It is not revellers, senhora, it's not! They are shouting 'death to Dr Bacamarte!!! The tyrant!'" said the frightened boy.

"Shut your mouth, fool! Benedita, look here at the left side; do you not find the stitching a touch askew? The blue stripe does not go all the way down; it is ugly like this; it will need to be unstitched to make it all just the same and . . ."

"Death to Dr Bacamarte!!! Death to the tyrant!" yelled three hundred voices outside. It was the rebellion flowing onto Rua Nova.

Every drop of blood drained from D. Evarista's face. For a moment she did not take a single step, did not move a single muscle; the fear petrified her. The maid ran instinctively to the back door. As for the slave boy, whom D. Evarista had doubted, he had a brief moment of triumph, a movement – sudden, imperceptible, deeply ingrained – of moral satisfaction, to see that reality had come to swear by him.

"Death to the alienist!" shouted the voices, closer now.

If D. Evarista could not easily resist the tempestuous lures of pleasure, she did at least know how to face up to moments of danger. She did not faint. She ran to the inner room where her husband was at his studies. When she rushed in, the distinguished doctor was scrutinising a text by Averroes; his eyes, dull with contemplation, rose from the book to the ceiling and fell back from the ceiling to the book, blind to external reality, seers to his profound mental work. D. Evarista called out to her husband twice, without his taking any notice of her; the third call he heard and he asked what the matter was, if she was sick.

"Can you not hear those cries?" his worthy wife asked tearfully.

Now the alienist took notice; the cries were getting closer, terrible, threatening; he understood everything. He got up from the straight high-backed chair where he had been sitting, shut the book and, his steps firm and calm, he walked over and placed it on the shelf. Since the introduction of the volume slightly broke the line of the two adjacent tomes, Simão Bacamarte took care to correct this defect that was tiny and yet actually rather interesting. Then he told his wife to withdraw, to do nothing.

"No, no!" the worthy lady implored him, "I want to die beside you . . ."

Simão Bacamarte insisted that, oh no, this was not a question of dying; and even if it were, he ordered her, in the name of life, to stay. The wretched woman bowed her head, obedient and tearful.

"Down with the Casa Verde!" shouted the Porridge Rebels.

The alienist went out onto the front balcony, arriving there at the very moment that the rebellion also arrived and stopped, right outside, its three hundred heads blazing with public-spiritedness and sombre with rage. "Death! Death!" they cried from all directions, the moment the figure of the alienist appeared on the balcony. Simão Bacamarte gestured that he wished to speak; the rebellious masses drowned his voice out with cries of indignation. Then, waving his hat to impose silence on the crowd, the barber managed to calm his friends, and informed the alienist that he might speak, though adding that he ought not to abuse the people's patience as he had hitherto.

"I shall say little, or indeed nothing at all, if that is required. I only wish to know first what it is that you ask for."

"We ask for nothing," replied the barber, shaking with anger. "We order that the Casa Verde be demolished, or at least that it be emptied of the poor souls within."

"I do not understand."

"You understand me well enough, tyrant; we want to restore to their freedom all the victims of your hatred, your whims, your greed . . ."

The alienist smiled, but this great man's smile was not something that the eyes of the crowd could see; it was a slight contraction of two or three muscles, no more. He smiled and replied:

"Gentlemen, science is a serious matter, and deserves to be treated seriously. I justify my actions as an alienist to nobody but some other learned experts and God. If you wish to propose amending the management of the Casa Verde, I am ready to hear you; but if you are demanding that I deny myself, you will gain nothing. I could invite some of you, under commission from the rest, to come take a look at the crazy inmates; but I do not, for that would be to justify my system to you, which I will not do, not to laymen and not to rebels."

So spoke the alienist, and the crowd was astonished; it was clear that they had not expected such energy, let alone such serenity. But the amazement grew further still when the alienist, bowing to the crowd with much gravity, turned his back and withdrew slowly into the house. At once the barber returned to his senses and, waving his hat, invited his friends to demolish the Casa Verde; a few weak voices answered him. It was at this decisive moment that the barber felt the ambition for government sprouting up within himself; it seemed to him that, by demolishing the Casa Verde and thwarting the alienist's influence, he would end up taking control of the Town Council, dominating the other authorities and setting himself up as lord of Itaguaí. For some years he had striven to see his name included on the pelouros for the drawing of councilmen, but he was turned down for not having a position compatible with such a major role. It was now or never. He had gone so far in the riots that defeat would be prison, or perhaps the gallows, or exile. Unfortunately, the alienist's response had diminished his followers' fury. The barber, on realising this, felt a surge of outrage, and he wanted to shout: "Rogues! Cowards!" but he contained himself and instead broke forth thus:

"My friends, let us struggle to the end! The salvation of Itaguaí is in your worthy, heroic hands. Let us destroy the prison of your children and parents, of your mothers and sisters, of your relatives and friends, indeed of you yourselves. Or you shall perish on a diet of bread and water, or under the whip, in that scoundrel's dungeon."

And the crowd shifted, murmured, shouted, threatened, gathered all around the barber. It was the revolt that was once again coming to, after its slight fainting spell, and that now threatened the destruction of the Casa Verde.

"Let's go!" shouted Porfírio, waving his hat.

"Let's go!" they all repeated.

A new occurrence prevented them: it was a corps of dragoons who, at double-time, were entering Rua Nova.

CHAPTER VII
THE UNEXPECTED

W HEN THE DRAGOONS appeared before the Porridge Rebels there was a moment of astonishment: the rebels could not believe that public enforcement had been sent out against them; but the barber understood everything, and he waited. The dragoons came to a halt, and their captain enjoined the crowd to disperse; but, although one part of them was so inclined, the rest strongly supported the barber, who replied in these lofty terms:

"No, we shall never disperse. If you would have our corpses, you may take them; but our corpses alone; you shall not take our honour, our reputation, our rights, and with them the salvation of Itaguaí."

Nothing could have been more reckless than this response from the barber; and nothing more natural. That is the dizziness that comes with major crises. Perhaps it was also an excess of confidence that the dragoons would show restraint; a confidence that the captain immediately dispelled, ordering them to charge on the Porridge Rebels. The moment was indescribable. The throng roared, furious; some of them, climbing through the windows of the houses or fleeing down the road, managed to escape; but the majority remained, puffing with anger, outraged, galvanised by the barber's grand exhortation. The Porridge Rebels' defeat was looking imminent when one third of the dragoons – whatever the reason for this, the town chronicles did not report it – moved suddenly to the side of the rebellion. These unexpected reinforcements gave heart to the Porridge Rebels, while simultaneously striking discouragement into the ranks of law and order. The loyal soldiers did not have the courage to attack their own fellows, and one by one they shifted gradually over to side with them, such that within a few minutes, the picture was looking quite different. The captain was on one side, with some people, standing against a compact mass threatening him with death. There was no remedy; he accepted defeat and surrendered his sword to the barber.

The triumphant revolution did not waste a minute; it carried the wounded to nearby houses and set off towards the Council chamber. Populace and troops were fraternising, giving cheers of God save His Majesty, and the viceroy, and Itaguaí, and "noble Porfirio". This man was up in front, wielding his sword so deftly it was as if it were merely a razor that happened to be a little longer than usual. Victory encircled his brow with a mysterious aura. His every sinew was starting to stiffen with the dignity of government.

The councilmen, at the windows, seeing the crowds and the troops, immediately determined that the troops had seized control of the crowds and, with no further examination, they went inside and voted to petition the viceroy that one month's pay be given to the dragoons, "whose boldness saved Itaguaí from the abyss into which it had been cast by a pack of rebels". This was the wording proposed by Sebastião Freitas, the dissident councilman, the one whose defence of the Porridge Rebels had so scandalised his colleagues. But very quickly the illusion came apart. All the long-lifes-to-the-barber, and the deaths-to-the-councilmen and to-the-alienist, brought news of the sad reality. The president did not lose heart: "Be our luck as it may," he said, "let us always remember that one is at the service of His Majesty and of the people." Sebastião implied that he could better serve the crown and the town by slipping out of the back door and going to confer with the itinerant judge, but the whole Council rejected this suggestion.

In no time at all, the barber, accompanied by some of his lieutenants, entered the chamber, and notified the Council of their fall. The Council offered no resistance, they handed themselves over and were led off to the prison. Then the barber's friends proposed that he assume the governing of the town, in His Majesty's name. Porfirio accepted the charge, even though he was not unfamiliar with (he added) the thorns it brought with it; he said moreover that he would depend on the cooperation of his friends present; to which they promptly agreed. The barber went to the window and communicated these resolutions to the people, which the people ratified, acclaiming him. He took on the designation of "Protector of the town in the name of His Majesty and the people". Many important orders were quickly despatched, and communications from the new government, a detailed report to the viceroy, with many protestations of obedience to His Majesty's orders; and finally a proclamation to the people, which was brief but vigorous:

Itaguaians!

A corrupt and violent Town Council was conspiring against the interests of His Majesty and the people. Public opinion condemned it; a handful of citizens, with the strong support of His Majesty's brave dragoons, has just dissolved it in ignominy; and by the town's unanimous consensus, I have been entrusted with the supreme command, until such time as His Majesty resolves to order whatever he may deem best for his royal service. Itaguaians! I ask nothing of you but that you encircle me in your trust, that you assist me in restoring peace and the public exchequer, which has been so ruined by the Council that is now terminated by your hands. Count upon my sacrifice, and be assured that the crown will be for us.

Protector of the town
in the name of His Majesty and the people
PORFÍRIO CAETANO DAS NEVES

Everybody noticed this proclamation's absolute silence on the matter of the Casa Verde; and according to some, there could be no livelier clue as to the barber's dark plans. The danger was all the greater because, in the midst of these grave events, the alienist had put another seven or eight people into the Casa Verde, among them two ladies, and one of the men being related to the Protector. It was not a provocation, an intentional act; but everyone interpreted it in that way, and the town breathed easier in the hope that within twenty-four hours the alienist would be in irons and the terrible prison destroyed.

The day ended joyfully. While the rattle-crier recited the proclamation from corner to corner, the people spread through the streets and swore to die in defence of noble Porfirio. There were some few shouts against the Casa Verde, proof of their confidence in the government's action. The barber had an act issued declaring the day a holiday, and broached a negotiation with the vicar for the celebrating of a Te Deum service, so convenient was the conjunction of temporal and spiritual power in his eyes; but Father Lopes turned his offer down flat.

"In any case, I trust that Your Reverence will not be joining the ranks of the government's enemies?"

To which Father Lopes replied, without replying:

"How could I join their ranks, if the new government has no enemies?"

The barber smiled; it was no more than the truth. Apart from the captain, the councilmen and the most prominent citizens of the town, everybody was offering him their support. And even if those same worthies did not support him publicly, nor had they come out against him. None of the almotacés failed to appear to receive their orders. All across the town, families were blessing the name of the man who would at last free Itaguaí from the Casa Verde and the terrible Simão Bacamarte.

CHAPTER VIII
THE APOTHECARY'S DISTRESS

TWENTY-FOUR HOURS AFTER the events recounted in the preceding chapter, the barber left the palace of government – this being the name given to the Council building – with two aides-de-camp, and set out towards the home of Simão Bacamarte. He was well aware that it would have been more dignified for the government to summon him; however, his fear that the alienist would not comply obliged him to appear tolerant and moderate.

I will not describe the apothecary's terror on hearing that the barber was going to the alienist's house. "He's going to arrest him," he thought. And his distress was redoubled. Indeed, the apothecary's moral torment in those revolutionary days exceeds all possible description. Never had a man felt himself in a tighter position – the alienist's friendship called him over to his side, the barber's victory drew him to the barber. The simple news of the uprising had already shaken his soul greatly, for he knew how unanimous was the hatred towards the alienist; but the final victory was also the final blow. His wife, a virile lady and a personal friend of D. Evarista's, told him that his place was beside Simão Bacamarte, while his heart cried out no, that the alienist's cause was lost, and that nobody, voluntarily, ties themselves to a corpse. "Cato did it, this is true, *sed victa Catoni*," he thought, recollecting some of Father Lopes's regular sermons, "but Cato did not bind himself to a lost cause, he was the lost cause himself, the cause of the republic; his act, therefore, was the act of a selfish man, of a self-ish wretch; my own situation is different." With his wife so insistent, however, Crispim Soares could find no other solution to this crisis than to fall ill; he announced that he was ill and he took to his bed.

"There goes Porfirio to Dr Bacamarte's house," said his wife the following day at his bedside. "He has people with him."

"He is going to arrest him," thought the apothecary.

One idea leads to another; and the apothecary imagined that, as soon as the alienist had been arrested, they would come for him, too, in his capacity as accomplice. This idea acted faster than any blister-agent. Crispim Soares got up, said that he was feeling quite well now, that he was going out; and despite all his consort's efforts and protestations, he dressed and went out. The old chroniclers are unanimous when they report that the certainty that her husband was going to position himself nobly at the alienist's side gave the apothecary's wife great consolation; and they note, most perceptively, the vast moral power of a delusion; for the apothecary walked resolutely to the palace of government, not to the alienist's house. On his arrival, he looked surprised not to find the barber, to whom he had intended to present his protestations of support, having not done so the previous day owing to his illness. And he coughed rather effortfully. The senior officials who heard this declaration of his, aware of the apothecary's closeness to the alienist, understood the full significance of this new support and they treated Crispim Soares most warmly; they informed him that the barber would not be long; His Lordship had gone to the Casa Verde, some important business, but he would not be long. They gave him a chair to sit on, and refreshments, and praise; they told him that noble Porfirio's cause was that of all patriots; to which the apothecary kept repeating, yes, he had never thought otherwise, that he would declare this very thing even to His Majesty.

CHAPTER IX
TWO LOVELY CASES

THE ALIENIST DID not delay in receiving the barber; he said he had no means of resisting, and he was thus ready to comply. He asked one thing only, that he not be compelled to witness the Casa Verde's destruction personally.

"Your Lordship is mistaken," said the barber after a pause, "you are mistaken in attributing intentions of vandalism to the government. Rightly or wrongly, public opinion is of the belief that most of the lunatics held in that place are in their perfect minds, but the government recognises that the question is a purely scientific one and would not contemplate resolving scientific questions with municipal ordinances. Furthermore, the Casa Verde is a public institution; we accept it as such from the hands of the now dissolved Town Council. There is, however, as in fact there must be, an intermediate proposal that might restore some calm to the public spirit."

The alienist could barely disguise his amazement; he admitted that he had expected something different, the demolition of the mental hospital, his own arrest, exile, anything but . . .

"Your Lordship's amazement," the barber cut in gravely, "comes from not being mindful of the grave responsibility that the government bears. The people, seized with a blind piety that gives them a legitimate outrage in such a case, may demand a certain sequence of actions from the government; but the latter, with the responsibility that falls to them, ought not to carry these out, at least not in their entirety; such is the situation in which we find ourselves. The generous revolution which yesterday overthrew a Town Council that was reviled and corrupt has shouted for the demolition of the Casa Verde; but could it even occur to the government to eliminate madness? No. And if the government cannot eliminate it, is it at least well-placed to discern it, to recognise it? Also no; it is a question of science. Thus, on such a tricky matter, the government cannot, should not, does not want to do without Your Lordship's cooperation. What it asks you is that we do somehow give the people some measure of satisfaction. Let us unite, and the people will know to obey. One acceptable proposal, if Your Lordship does not suggest another, would be to have those patients removed from the Casa Verde who are almost cured and likewise the more trivially mad, etc. Thus, with no great danger, one might show a degree of tolerance and mercy."

"How many dead and wounded were there yesterday in the clashes?" asked Simão Bacamarte, about three minutes later.

The barber was surprised at the question, but he replied at once that there were eleven dead and twenty-five wounded.

"Eleven dead and twenty-five wounded!" the alienist repeated twice or thrice.

And he declared at once that the current proposal did not seem right to him, but that he would procure another, and in a few days he would give his answer. And he asked a number of questions about the previous day's events, the attack, defence, support of the dragoons, how the Council had resisted etc., to which the barber gave plentiful answers, insisting primarily upon the discredit into which the Council had fallen. The barber confessed that the new government did not yet have the confidence of the worthies of the town, but there was much that the alienist might do in this regard. The government, concluded the barber, would rest easier if it could count not yet on the affection but at least on the goodwill of the loftiest spirit of Itaguaí, and surely of the kingdom. But none of this altered the noble and austere expression of that great man, who listened without a word, with neither arrogance nor modesty, but impassive as a God of stone.

"Eleven dead and twenty-five wounded," repeated the alienist to himself after he had accompanied the barber to the door. "What we have here are two perfectly lovely cases of mental sickness. This barber's symptoms of duplicity and insolence are incontrovertible. As for the folly of those who cheered him, no further proof is needed than the eleven dead and twenty-five wounded. Two lovely cases!"

town's most decisive people around João Pina. Porfírio, seeing his old razor rival at the head of the insurrection, understood that his own loss was irredeemable if he did not strike a decisive blow; he issued two decrees, one of them abolishing the Casa Verde, the other exiling the alienist. João Pina clearly demonstrated, using grand words, that Porfírio's act was a simple device, a decoy, in which the people should not believe. Two hours later Porfírio fell ignominiously and João Pina took on the hard task of governing. Finding the draft of the proclamation in the files, along with the report to the viceroy and other inaugural acts by the previous government, he hurried to have them newly copied and issued; the chroniclers add, and besides one would assume as much, that he changed the names, and where the other barber had spoken of a corrupt Town Council, this one spoke of "an intruder riddled with evil French doctrines and quite contrary to the sacrosanct interests of His Majesty", etc.

At this point, a force despatched by the viceroy arrived in the town, and they re-established order. The alienist immediately demanded that the barber be handed over, and likewise fifty-something individuals whom he pronounced crazy; and not only did they give him these but they also pledged to hand over another nineteen of the barber's followers, who were convalescing from the wounds they had suffered in the first rebellion.

This moment in Itaguaí's crisis also marked the high point of Simão Bacamarte's influence. Whatever he wanted was given to him; and we can see one of the liveliest proofs of the distinguished doctor's power in just how readily the councilmen, restored to their positions, consented for Sebastião Freitas also to be taken into the mental hospital. The alienist, knowing of the extraordinary inconsistency of this councilman's views, had understood that he was a pathological case and put in a request for him. The same thing happened to the apothecary. As soon as the alienist was told about Crispim Soares's momentary support for the Porridge Rebellion, he compared this to the approval he had always received from him, even the very day before, and had him taken. Crispim Soares did not deny the event, but explained that he had yielded to an impulse of terror, on seeing the rebellion triumphant, and offered in evidence the lack of any other actions on his part, adding that he had gone straight back to bed, ill. Simão Bacamarte did not contradict him; he told the onlookers, however, that terror is also the father of madness, and that the case of Crispim Soares seemed to him one of the most exemplary.

But the clearest proof of Simão Bacamarte's influence was the docility with which the Town Council handed over their president himself. This worthy legislator had declared, mid-session, that he was not satisfied to wash away the offence of the Porridge Rebels with fewer than thirty almudes of blood; words that reached the alienist's ear from the mouth of the Council secretary, who was filled with enthusiasm. Simão Bacamarte began by putting the secretary into the Casa Verde, and proceeded thence to the Council chamber, where he declared that the president was suffering from "bulls' dementia", a type he intended to study, to the great benefit of the population. The Council hesitated at first, but ultimately yielded.

From then onwards, it was unbridled harvest. A man could not devise or disseminate the simplest lie in the world, even one of those that might benefit the inventor or spreader himself, without being put straight into the Casa Verde. Everything was madness. The cultivators of riddles, the makers of puzzles, of anagrams, the slanderers, those who took excessive interest in the lives of others, dandies who put all their care into their dress, the occasional puffed-up almotacé, nobody escaped the alienist's emissaries. He respected lovers and did not spare flirts, saying that the former were giving in to a natural impulse and the latter to a vice. If a man was miserly or profligate, he would go to the Casa Verde just the same; hence the allegation that there were no rules for perfect mental sanity. Some chroniclers believe that Simão Bacamarte did not always proceed openly, and they quote in corroboration of this statement (the validity of which I am unable to confirm) the fact of his having managed to attain from the Council a municipal order authorising the use of a silver ring on the thumb of the left hand for all people who, without any other documentary or traditional proof, claimed to have two or three ounces of Goth blood in their veins. These chroniclers say that the secret purpose of his proposal to the Council was the enrichment of a jeweller, a good friend of his; but, although it was true that the jeweller did see his business prosper in the wake of the new municipal order, it was no less so that the order in question also gave the Casa Verde a whole crowd of tenants; for which reason, it is not possible to define, without risk of foolhardiness, our esteemed doctor's true aims. As for the determining reason for the capture and housing in the Casa Verde of all those who wore the ring, it is one of the obscurest points in Itaguaí's history; the most credible opinion is that these people were taken in for having wandered around gesticulating, randomly, on the streets, at

One day, I am sure Your Reverence will recall it, she proposed making a new dress each year for the image of Our Lady at the mother church. All these were serious symptoms; last night, however, complete insanity revealed itself. She had chosen, prepared, adorned the outfit that she would be wearing to the Town Council's ball; she was just wavering between a garnet necklace and a sapphire one. The night before last, she asked me which she should wear; I replied that either would look good on her. Yesterday she repeated the question over lunch; not long after the meal, I found her quiet and thoughtful. 'What is the matter?' I asked her. 'I wanted to wear the garnet necklace, but I do think the sapphire one so very beautiful!' 'Then wear the sapphire one.' 'Oh, but what to do about the garnet?' Finally she spent the whole evening with no great change. We dined, and retired to bed. In the depths of the night, it must have been one-thirty, I wake up and I cannot see her; I rise from my bed, I go to her closet, I find her back at the two necklaces, trying them out in the looking-glass, now one, now the other. The derangement was obvious; I took her in at once."

The answer did not satisfy Father Lopes, but he made no objection. The alienist, however, observed this and explained that D. Evarista's was a case of "sumptuary mania", which was not incurable, and in any case was worthy of study.

"I expect to make her well within six weeks," he concluded.

And the distinguished doctor's self-denial enhanced him greatly. Conjectures, inventions, suspicions, everything crumbled to the ground since he had not hesitated to take his own wife into the Casa Verde, his wife whom he loved with all the strength of his soul. No one else had any right to resist him – still less to attribute any intent to him beyond science.

He was an austere, great man, Hippocrates and Cato in one.

CHAPTER XI
THE ASTONISHMENT OF ITAGUAÍ

AT THIS POINT the reader would do well to prepare himself for the same astonishment into which the town fell, on learning one day that all the mad people in the Casa Verde were to be turned out onto the street.

"All of them?"

"All of them."

"Impossible; some of them, yes, but all of them . . ."

"All of them. That is what he said in the letter he sent the Town Council this morning."

Indeed, the alienist had notified the Council, explaining: 1st, that he had checked the statistics for the town and for the Casa Verde, and that at the current time, four-fifths of the population were housed in that establishment; 2nd, that this transfer of population had given him cause to examine the fundamental principles of his theory of brain illnesses, a theory that excluded from the domain of reason all those cases where the faculties were not in perfect and absolute equilibrium; 3rd, that this examination and this statistical fact had led to his conviction that the true doctrine was rather the reverse, and thus that the imbalance of faculties should be allowed as normal and all cases where equilibrium was uninterrupted as pathological; 4th, that, in view of this, he was notifying the Council that he would release the Casa Verde's inmates and gather within it all those who found themselves in the conditions herein described; 5th, that in his attempts to discover scientific truth, he would not spare his efforts of any kind, expecting the like dedication from the Council; 6th, that he would restore to the Council and to individuals the sum total of the stipend received for the housing of the supposed lunatics, deducting the part actually spent on food, clothing, etc., which the

Council might check in the Casa Verde's books and coffers.

Itaguaí's astonishment was great; the joy of the inmates' relatives and friends was no less. Dinners, dances, illuminations, music, there was everything in celebration of such a fortuitous event. I do not describe the festivities because they are not to our purpose; but they were splendid, moving and protracted.

And such are the things of mankind! Amidst the rejoicing prompted by Simão Bacamarte's official letter, nobody noticed the last line of item the 4th, a phrase that was full of future experiments.

CHAPTER XII
THE LAST PART OF ITEM THE 4TH

THE ILLUMINATIONS WERE extinguished, families were reconstituted, everything seemed to have been restored to its former axis. Order reigned, the Town Council was governing once again, with no external pressure; the president himself and councilman Freitas returned to their positions. The barber Porfirio, who had learned from events, having "tasted everything", as the poet said of Napoleon, and more besides, for Napoleon had not tasted the Casa Verde, the barber thought the obscure glory of razor and scissors preferable to the dazzling calamities of power; he was prosecuted, it is true; but the town's population begged His Majesty's clemency; hence the pardon. João Pina was acquitted, in acknowledgement of the fact that he had unseated a rebel. The chroniclers believe this to be the origin of our old adage: a thief who robs a thief gets a hundred years' relief – an adage that is immoral, truth be told, but tremendously useful.

Not only did the complaints against the alienist stop, but not even resentment remained for the actions he had taken; in addition to which, the inmates of the Casa Verde, ever since he had declared them to be in perfect reason, felt themselves seized by a deep gratitude and fervent enthusiasm. Many understood that the alienist deserved some especial display, and they gave him a ball, which was followed by other balls and dinners. The town chronicles report that D. Evarista initially had the notion of parting from her consort, but the pain of losing the company of such a great man defeated any personal grievance, and the couple ended up even happier than before.

No less intimate was the friendship between the alienist and the apothecary. The latter concluded from Simão Bacamarte's official missive that prudence is the greatest of virtues in times of revolution, and was most appreciative of the magnanimity of the alienist who, upon granting him his freedom, held out a hand in enduring friendship.

"He is a great man," he said to his wife, referring to that incident.

No need to speak of the saddler, of Costa, of Coelho, of Martim Brito and others, those named particularly in this text; suffice it to say that they were able freely to exercise their former customs. Martim Brito himself, previously locked up for a speech in which he had enthusiastically praised D. Evarista, now made another in honour of the eminent doctor, "whose most lofty genius, its wings surging far up above the sun, left beneath it all other spirits of the earth".

"I thank you for your words," the alienist answered, "and still I do not regret having restored to you your freedom."

The Council that had responded to Simão Bacamarte's official letter with the proviso that they would in due course legislate in relation to the last part of item the 4th, did at last try to pass legislation about it. Without any debate, a municipal order was adopted authorising the alienist to welcome into the Casa Verde those people who believed themselves to be enjoying perfect equilibrium of their mental faculties. And because the Council's experiences had been painful, they established a clause by which the authorisation was provisional, limited to one year, intending that the new psychological theory might be tested out, with the Council empowered, even before that time was up, to order the closure of the Casa Verde, if it were deemed advisable for reasons of public order. Councilman Freitas also proposed a declaration that in no case would councilmen be taken into the asylum of the mad: a clause that was accepted, voted on and included in the order, despite councilman Galvão's objections. The main argument put forward by this legislator being that the Council, legislating on a scientific experiment, cannot exclude the persons of its members from the consequences of that law; any such exception was odious and ridiculous. No sooner had he uttered these two words than the other councilmen broke out in loud cries against their colleague's audacity and folly; he, however, listened to them and merely said that he intended to vote against the exemption.

"Councillorship," he concluded, "does not endow us with any especial powers, nor does it exempt us from humanity."

Simão Bacamarte accepted the municipal order with all its restrictions. As for the exclusion of the councilmen, he declared that he would regret it terribly if he were compelled to take them into the Casa Verde; the clause, however, was the best possible proof that they did not suffer from a perfect equilibrium to their mental faculties. The same could not be said for councilman Galvão, whose correctness in the objection that he had raised, and whose moderation in responding to his colleagues' diatribes, showed a well-organised brain on his part; for which reason he asked the Council to surrender him up. Feeling injured yet at councilman Galvão's conduct, the Council looked favourably on the alienist's request, and voted unanimously to hand him over.

Now, let it be understood that, according to the new theory, one deed or saying was not enough to take somebody into the Casa Verde; a protracted examination was required, a vast enquiry into his past and present. Father Lopes, for example, was only captured thirty days after the municipal order, the apothecary's wife after forty. The locking up of this particular lady filled her spouse with great indignation. Crispim Soares left his house seething with rage, declaring to all he met that he would tear the tyrant's ears off. One fellow, an opponent of the alienist's, upon hearing this news on the street, forgot the reasons for his dissidence and ran to Simão Bacamarte's house to notify him of the danger he was in. Simão Bacamarte showed his gratitude for his opponent's behaviour, and it took him only minutes to recognise the rectitude of the man's sentiments, his good faith, his respect for humanity, his generosity; he shook both his hands heartily, and took him into the Casa Verde.

"Cases like his are rare," he said to his astonished wife. "Now let us await our friend Crispim."

Crispim Soares came in. His sorrow had overcome his rage now, and the apothecary did not rip the alienist's ears off. The latter consoled his friend, assuring him that it was not a lost cause; maybe his wife did have some kind of brain trouble; he would examine her most attentively; but until then, he could not leave her on the streets. And, since he thought it beneficial to reunite them, because the husband's cunning and deceit might somehow cure the moral beauty he had discovered in the wife, Simão Bacamarte said:

"You, senhor, will work in your pharmacy during the day, but will take lunch and dinner with your wife, and you will spend your nights, your Sundays, and your holy days here."

The proposal put the unfortunate apothecary in the position of Buridan's ass. He wanted to live with his wife, but feared returning to the Casa Verde; and he remained in this struggle for some time, until

D. Evarista released him from his quandary, promising that she would take it upon herself to visit her friend in the asylum and would convey messages between the two of them. Crispim Soares kissed her hands in gratitude. How sublime this final stroke of cowardly selfishness was, thought the alienist.

After five months, some eighteen people had been lodged in the Casa Verde; but Simão Bacamarte did not slacken; he would go from street to street, from house to house, looking, questioning, studying; and whenever he picked up someone sick, he would take them away with the same joy with which formerly he had gathered them up by the dozen. This same disproportion confirmed the new theory; he had at last found the true brain pathology. One day, he managed to put the itinerant judge into the Casa Verde; but he proceeded with such scrupulousness that he only did so after studying all the man's actions in the tiniest detail, and questioning the worthies of the town. More than once, he was about to take in people who in fact were perfectly unbalanced; that was what happened with a lawyer, in whom he recognised such a collection of moral and mental qualities that it would have been dangerous to leave him out on the street. He ordered that the man be taken; but his agent, doubtful, asked if he might first conduct an experiment; he called on a good friend, who was being sued for having falsified a will, and advised him to engage Salustiano as his lawyer; that was the name of the person in question.

"So you really think . . .?"

"No doubt about it. Go, confess everything to him, the whole truth, whatever it might be, and entrust the case to him."

The man called on the lawyer, confessed that he had falsified the will, and ended up asking him to take on the case. The lawyer did not deny him; he studied the briefs, and argued at length, proving beyond a shadow of a doubt that the will was more than truthful. The defendant's innocence was solemnly proclaimed by the judge and the inheritance passed into his hands. The distinguished jurist owed his freedom to this experiment. But nothing escapes an original and incisive mind. Simão Bacamarte, who had for some time been observing that agent's zeal, shrewdness, patience and moderation, recognised the skill and discernment with which he had completed such a tricky and elaborate experiment, and determined that he should be taken at once into the Casa Verde; he did, however, give him one of the very best cells.

The inmates were housed by class. One gallery was made up of the modest; that is, those lunatics in whom this was the moral perfection that predominated;

another of the tolerant, another of the truthful, another of the trusting, another of the loyal, another of the magnanimous, another of the wise, another of the honest, etc. Naturally, the inmates' families and friends railed against the theory; and some attempted to force the Council to revoke the permit. The Council, however, had not forgotten the language of councilman Galvão, and if they revoked the permit, they would see him out again and restored to his position; for which reason, they refused. Simão Bacamarte wrote the councilmen an official letter, not thanking them, but congratulating them on this act of personal vendetta.

Disillusioned at the workings of legality, some of the town worthies called in secret on the barber Porfirio and pledged him every support they could, in people, in money and in influence at court, if he were to place himself at the head of another movement against the Town Council and the alienist. The barber said no; he said that overweening ambition had led him to break the law the first time, but that he had mended his ways, acknowledging his own mistake and the inconstant opinion of his own followers; that the Council had resolved to authorise the alienist's new experiment, for one year: so they should either wait for the end of the allotted time, or petition the viceroy, in the event that the Council itself rejected their request.

He would never advise the employment of a measure that he had seen fail in his hands, and this at the cost of deaths and injuries that would be his eternal regret.

"What are you saying?" asked the alienist when a covert agent told him of the conversation between the barber and the citizens.

Two days later, the barber was taken into the Casa Verde. "Damned if I do, damned if I don't!" the unfortunate man exclaimed.

The allotted time came to an end, and the Town Council authorised an extension period of six months for the testing of therapeutic measures. The outcome of this episode in the Itaguaian chronicles is on such a scale, and so unexpected, that it should deserve no fewer than ten chapters of exposition; but I shall content myself with one, which will be the conclusion of the narrative, and one of the most beautiful examples of scientific conviction and human self-denial.

CHAPTER XIII
PLUS ULTRA!

I T WAS THERAPY'S turn. Simão Bacamarte, so active and shrewd in the discovering of patients, outdid himself in the diligence and insight with which he began to treat them. On this point all the chroniclers entirely agree: the esteemed alienist carried out astonishing cures, arousing the liveliest admiration in Itaguaí.

Indeed, it was hard to imagine a more rational therapeutic system. The lunatics being divided by class, according to the particular moral perfection that in each of them exceeded all others, Simão Bacamarte took care to attack this predominant quality head-on. Take, say, a man of modesty. Bacamarte would administer the medication that might instil the opposite feeling in him; and he would not go straight to the maximum dosage – he would regulate it, according to the patient's condition, age, temperament and social status. Sometimes a tailcoat was enough, or a ribbon, a wig, a cane, to restore reason to the mad; in other cases, the trouble was more unruly; he would then have recourse to diamond rings, to honorific distinctions, etc. There was one sick man, a poet, who held out against everything. Simão Bacamarte began to despair of curing him, when he had the idea of getting the rattle going, to proclaim the man a rival to Garção and Pindar.

"It was a blessed remedy," the unfortunate man's mother told a dear friend. "It was a blessed remedy."

Another sick man, likewise modest, put up the same resistance to the medication; but not being a writer (he could barely sign his name), the rattle remedy could not be applied to him. It occurred to Simão Bacamarte to request that the man be named secretary to the Itaguaí's Academy of the Protected. The posts of president and secretaries were conferred by royal appointment, by the especial grace of the late king Dom João V, and entailed the styling of Excellency and the wearing of a gold badge on one's hat. The government in Lisbon refused to grant the appointment; but since the alienist argued that he was not requesting it as an honorary award of a legitimate distinction, but only as a means of therapy for a tricky case, the government acquiesced exceptionally to the request; and even then, they only did so thanks to an extraordinary effort by the Minister of the Navy and Overseas Territories, who happened to be the alienist's cousin. Another blessed remedy.

"Truly, it is marvellous!" people said on the street, when they beheld the healthy and puffed-up expressions of the two ex-madmen.

So went the system. The rest can be imagined. Each moral or mental beauty was attacked at the very place where the perfection seemed most solid; and the effect was sure. Though it was not sure always. There were cases where the preeminent quality was resistant to everything; then the alienist would attack some other part, applying to therapy the methods of military strategy, which will take a fortress at one point if it cannot breach it at another.

After five and a half months, the Casa Verde was empty; all cured! Councilman Galvão, so cruelly afflicted with moderation and equity, had the good fortune to lose an uncle; I say good fortune, for the uncle left a will that was ambiguous, and the councilman secured a favourable interpretation by bribing the judges and hoodwinking the other heirs. The alienist's honesty was seen in this instance; he confessed candidly that he had played no part in this cure: it was the simple *vis medicatrix naturae*. The same did not occur in Father Lopes's case. As the alienist knew that the priest was altogether ignorant of Hebrew and Greek, he charged him to carry out a critical analysis of the Septuagint; the priest accepted the task, and he did it in good time; two months later, he had a book and his freedom. As for the apothecary's wife, she was not long in the cell that had been assigned to her, and where in fact she seldom wanted for attention.

"Why does Crispim not come to visit me?" she would ask daily.

They would answer her now this, now that; finally they told her the whole truth. The worthy matron could not contain her outrage and shame. In her explosions of rage, many disparate fragments of expressions escaped from her lips, such as these:

"Rascal! ... Crook! ... Scoundrel! ... A rogue who has built his wealth on fake and rotten ointments ... Oh – the rascal!"

Simão Bacamarte noticed that, even though the accusation that these words contained was not true, they were enough to demonstrate that the fine lady was at last restored to a perfect imbalance of her faculties; and he promptly discharged her.

Now, if you imagine that the alienist was overjoyed at the sight of the last guest leaving the Casa Verde, you are thereby revealing that you still do not know our man. *Plus ultra!* was his slogan. It was not enough for him to have discovered the true theory of madness; it did not content him that he had established the kingdom of reason in Itaguaí. *Plus ultra!* He was not happy, he was troubled, contemplative; something was telling him that the new theory had, within itself, another extremely new theory.

"Let us see," he thought. "Let us see if I might reach the ultimate truth at last."

He would say this, as he walked the length of the huge room, in which there blazed the richest library anywhere in His Majesty's overseas dominions. A broad damask robe, tied at the waist with a silk cord, with gold tassels (a gift from a University) enveloped the distinguished alienist's majestic and austere body. The wig covered a large and noble bald patch that he had acquired in his everyday contemplation of science. His feet, neither slim and feminine, nor big and oafish, but quite in proportion to his figure, were protected by a pair of shoes whose buckles were no more than simple and modest brass. Behold the difference: luxuriousness in him could only be seen in what was of scientific origin; what came from himself bore the tenor of moderation and simplicity, virtues so well-suited to the person of a learned man.

Thus went he, the great alienist, from one end of the vast library to the other, lost in his thoughts, far removed from anything that was not the dark problem of brain pathology. Suddenly, he stopped. Standing there, beside a window, with his left elbow resting in his right hand, palm open, and his chin on his left hand, which was closed, he asked himself:

"But were they truly insane, and cured by me – or was what appeared to be a cure no more than the discovery of the perfect imbalance of their brains?"

And burrowing down from there, you have the result at which he arrived: the well-organised brains that he had just cured were unbalanced like all the rest. Yes, he said to himself, I cannot claim to have instilled some feeling in them or some new faculty; both things already existed, perhaps only in a latent form, but exist they did.

Having reached this conclusion, the distinguished alienist had two contrary sensations, one of pleasure, the other of dejection. The one of pleasure was at seeing that, after long and patient investigations, ceaseless work, tremendous struggles with the townspeople, he could assert this truth: there were no mad people in Itaguaí; Itaguaí did not possess a single lunatic. But as quickly as this idea had refreshed his soul, another appeared to neutralise the first effect; it was the idea of doubt. What then! Did Itaguaí not possess one single well-corrected brain? Would not this conclusion, being so absolute, thus be mistaken, and would it not therefore destroy the whole broad and majestic edifice of the new psychological doctrine?

The anguish of the distinguished Simão Bacamarte is defined by the Itaguaian chroniclers as one of the most frightful moral storms ever to have poured down on man. But only the weak are felled by storms; the strong stiffen against them and stare down the thunder. Twenty minutes later, the alienist's features lit up with a gentle clarity.

"Yes, that must be it," he thought.

And it was this. Simão Bacamarte found within himself the characteristics of perfect mental and moral equilibrium; it seemed to him that he possessed the wisdom, the patience, the perseverance, the tolerance, the truthfulness, the moral vigour, the loyalty, in short, all the qualities that might make up a consummate lunatic. He did immediately doubt himself, it is true, and even concluded that it was mere illusion; but, being a prudent man, he resolved to convene a council of his friends, whom he questioned frankly. Their opinion was affirmative.

"No defects?"

"None," replied the assembled group in chorus.

"No vices?"

"None."

"Everything perfect?"

"Everything."

"But no, it's impossible," cried the alienist. "I tell you, I cannot feel within myself the superiority that I have just seen so splendidly defined. It is your affection that makes you speak thus. I study myself and find nothing to justify the excesses of your kindness."

The group insisted; the alienist resisted; finally Father Lopes explained everything with this worthy observation:

"Do you know the reason you cannot see your lofty qualities, which incidentally we do so admire? It is because you have one other quality that throws all the rest into relief: modesty."

This proved decisive. Simão Bacamarte bowed his head, at once joyful and sad, and even more joyful than sad. Immediately, he took himself into the Casa Verde. In vain did his wife and friends beseech him to stay, telling him that he was perfectly sane and balanced; neither entreaties nor suggestions nor tears detained him for a single moment.

"The question is a scientific one," he would say. "What it is, is a new doctrine, of which I am the first example. I combine both theory and practice within myself."

"Simão! Simão! My love!" cried his wife, her face washed with tears.

But the distinguished doctor, his eyes ablaze with scientific conviction, locked his ears to his dear wife's longing, and pushed her gently away. He shut the door of the Casa Verde, surrendering to the study and cure of himself. According to the chroniclers, he died seventeen months later, in the same condition in which he had entered, having failed to accomplish the least measure of progress. There are those who conjecture that there had never been any other mad person but he in Itaguaí, but this opinion, based upon a rumour that spread from the time of the alienist's decease, has nothing to prove it but the rumour itself; and a dubious rumour besides, since it is attributed to Father Lopes, who had himself emphasised the great man's qualities with such fervour. In any case, the burial was carried out with great pomp and uncommon solemnity.

THE LOOKING-GLASS
Sketch towards a new theory of the human soul

FOUR OR FIVE gentlemen were discussing, one night, certain questions of the greatest transcendence, the disparity in their views doing nothing to temper the mood. The house was on the Santa Teresa hill, the living-room was small, lit by candles whose glow blended mysteriously with the moonlight coming from outside. Between the city, with its disturbances and its thrills, and the sky, in which the stars blinked, through an atmosphere that was clear and calm, sat our four or five researchers into metaphysical matters, amicably resolving the most arduous problems of the universe.

Why four or five? If we are to be precise, there were four speaking; but, besides them, there was a fifth character in the living-room, silent, pensive, dozing, whose contribution to the debate never went beyond the occasional grunt of approval. This man was the same age as his companions, between forty and fifty; he was from the country, a capitalist, intelligent, not uneducated and, it would appear, shrewd and caustic. He never argued; and he defended his abstention with a paradox, saying that argument is the polished form of the fighting instinct, an instinct that man retains like a bestial inheritance; and he would add that the cherubim and seraphim never argued at all, and were they not, in fact, eternal and spiritual perfection? As he gave this usual response on that night, one of those present responded, challenging him to prove what he said, if he could. Jacobina (that was his name) considered for a moment, and replied:

"Now that I give it some more thought, senhor, you might be correct."

And then, in the middle of the night, it happened that this sullen fellow did take the floor, and not for two or three minutes but thirty or forty. The discussion, in its meanderings, had just landed on the nature of the soul, a topic that divided the four friends radically. To each head, a different view; not only was agreement difficult, but so was discussion itself, if not impossible, on account of the multiplicity of questions that branched out from the main trunk, and also partly, perhaps, on account of the inconsistency of the men's opinions. One of the debaters asked Jacobina if he had some opinion of his own, some conjecture, at least.

"No conjecture, and no opinion," he retorted. "Either one can give rise to disagreement, and, as you all know, I do not argue. But if you would care to listen in silence, I can tell you a story from my life that very clearly demonstrates the subject in question. In the first place, there is not just one soul, there are two . . ."

"Two?"

"No fewer than two souls. Every human creature has two souls: one looking from the inside outward, and the other from outside in . . . Be as amazed as you like, feel free to gawp, shrug, whatever you please; but I will not countenance any reply. If you talk back to me, I will finish my cigar and retire to bed. The external soul can be a spirit, a fluid, a man, several men, an object, an operation. There are cases, for instance, where a simple shirt button is somebody's external soul; and likewise the polka, a game of ombre, a book, a machine, a pair of boots, a cavatina, a drum, etc. It is clear that the role of this second soul is to transmit life, like the first; the pair of them complete the man, who is, metaphysically speaking, an orange. Anybody who loses one of the halves naturally loses half of his existence; and cases do exist, and they are not uncommon, in which the loss of the external soul implies that of the internal existence. Shylock, for example. That Jew's external soul was his ducats; losing them was equivalent to dying. I shall never see my gold again, he tells Tubal; *thou stickest a dagger in me.* Take good note of that line; the loss of his ducats, his external soul, was death to him. Now, it is important to know that the external soul does not always remain the same."

"It does not?"

"No, senhor; it changes in nature and in state. I am not referring to certain absorbent souls, like the fatherland, with which Camões said he would die, and power, which was Caesar's external soul and Cromwell's. These are potent, exclusive souls; but there are others, which, however potent, are changeable in nature. There are certain gentlemen, for example, whose external soul, in their early years, was a rattle or a hobbyhorse, and later, one might suppose, some charitable body. As for me, I know a lady – truly, a very dear one – who changes her external soul five, six times a year. During the season it is the opera; when the season ends, that external soul is replaced by another: a concert, a Cassino dance, the Rua do Ouvidor, the town of Petrópolis . . ."

"Excuse me, which lady is this?"

the post and these people had lost out. I suppose, also, that some part of the displeasure was entirely gratuitous: it was born from the simple distinction. I recall some lads, with whom I used to get along, starting to look at me askance, and this continued for some time. To compensate, I did have many people who were glad at the appointment; and the proof is that I received my whole uniform as a gift from friends. Then one of my aunts, D. Marcolina, the widow of Capt. Peçanha, who lived many leagues from our town, on a hidden and isolated little farm, wished to see me, and asked me to go to her and bring my uniform. I went, accompanied by a page, who days later returned to the town, because Aunt Marcolina, no sooner did she have me on the farm than she wrote to my mother saying she would not let me go before a month was up, if not longer. And she embraced me! She too called me her very own ensign. She thought me a handsome, strapping lad. Being rather frivolous in nature, she even confessed that she was jealous of the girl who would be my wife. She swore that in the whole province there could be none my equal. And it was nothing but ensign this, ensign that, constantly nothing but ensign. I asked her to call me Joãozinho, affectionately, like before; but she shook her head, crying oh no, that I was 'Senhor Ensign' now. An in-law of hers who lived there, the late

Peçanha's brother, addressed me no differently. I was 'Senhor Ensign', not in jest, but in all seriousness, and in full view of the slaves, who naturally followed that same path. At table I was seated at the best place, and I was first to be served. You cannot imagine. If I told you that Aunt Marcolina went so far as to order that a large looking-glass be placed in my room, a lavish, splendid object, quite out of keeping with the rest of the house, whose furniture was modest and simple . . . It was a looking-glass she had been given by her godmother, who had inherited it from her mother, who had bought it from one of the noblewomen who came over in 1808 with the court of D. João VI. I cannot say how much truth there was in this; but that was the tradition. The looking-glass was naturally very old; but some of the gold could still be seen in it, a little eaten away by time, with dolphins carved into the upper corners of the frame, mother-of-pearl embellishments and other whims of the artist's. All old, but very fine . . ."

"It was big?"

"Big, yes. And it was, like I said, a very great kindness, because the looking-glass had previously been in the living-room; it was the finest piece in the house. But nothing could sway her from her intention; she replied that she would not miss it, it would only be for a few weeks, and finally that 'Senhor Ensign' deserved this and so much more. The fact is, all those things, those affections, attentions, favours, they caused a transformation in me, which the natural feelings of youth encouraged and completed. You can imagine how, I suppose?"

"No."

"The ensign did away with the man. For a few days, the two natures remained in balance; but it was not long before the primal one yielded to the other; only the least part of humanity was left. It then happened that my external soul, which formerly had been the sun, the air, the countryside, the eyes of girls, changed in nature to become politeness and the bowings and scrapings of the household, everything that spoke to me of the position, nothing that spoke of the man. The only part that I retained of the citizen was the part that related to the exercising of the commission; the rest melted into the air and into the past. Hard to believe, is it not?"

"Hard even to understand," one of the hearers replied.

"But understand you shall. Actions can explain better than feelings; actions are everything. The best definition of love is worth less than a kiss on a beloved girl's lips; and, if I recall correctly, one ancient philosopher demonstrated motion by walking. So let us get to the actions. Let us see how, as the man's consciousness was being obliterated, the ensign's was becoming alive and intense. Human pains, human joys, if that was all they were, received barely a flicker of apathetic sympathy from me or a smile of favour. After three weeks, I was a different person, totally transformed. I was an ensign. Now, one day, Aunt Marcolina received grave news; one of her daughters, who was married to a labourer living five leagues away, was sick and soon to die. Farewell, nephew! Farewell, ensign! She was a doting mother, and arranged a journey right away, asking her brother-in-law to go with her, and me to take care of the farm. I believe that had it not been for her distressed state, she would have arranged the opposite; she would have left her brother-in-law and taken me. But the fact is that I was left alone, with only the few house slaves. I can admit that I soon felt a great oppression, an effect not unlike four prison walls being raised up suddenly around me. It was my external soul being reduced; this was limited now to a few uncouth creatures. The ensign continued to dominate in me, although life was less intense, and my awareness of it weaker. The slaves brought a note of humility into their courtesies, which did in part compensate for the familial affections and the afraid; I was rather brazen, in fact, so much so that I felt nothing, not for a few hours. I was sad at the harm caused to Marcolina; I was also somewhat perplexed, not knowing whether I ought to go to her, to convey the sad news, or to remain there taking care of the house. I opted for the second, so as not to leave the house abandoned, and also because, if my sick cousin was in a very bad way, I would only be adding to my aunt's maternal pain with no remedy; besides, I was expecting Uncle Peçanha's brother to return on that day or the next, seeing as he had already been gone thirty-six hours. But the morning passed with no trace of him; in the afternoon I began to feel like somebody who had lost all working of his nerves, as well as any sense of the workings of his muscles. Uncle Peçanha did not return that day, nor the next, nor anytime that week. My solitude assumed vast proportions. Never had the days been longer, never had the sun scorched the earth with a more wearisome persistence. The hours struck from one age to the next on the old living-room clock, whose pendular *tick-tock, tick-tock,* wounded my inner soul, like an unceasing fillip from eternity. When, many years later, I read an American poem, I believe it was by Longfellow, and encountered that famous refrain: *Forever – never! Never – forever!,* I confess I felt a shiver run down my spine: I recalled those captain or major; and all of that made me live. But when I woke, to a bright day, the awareness of my new unique being faded with my sleep – for then my inner soul lost its exclusivity of action, and was dependent on the other that insisted on not coming back . . . And it did not. I went outside, walked this way and that, hoping to see any sign of return. *Soeur Anne, soeur Anne, ne vois-tu rien venir?* Nothing, not a thing. Nothing but the dust of the road and the grass of the hills. I went back into the house, nervous, desperate, and stretched myself out on the living-room sofa. *Tick-tock, tick-tock.* I got up, wandered about, drummed on the window-panes, whistled. At one point I thought to write something, an article on politics, a novel, an ode; I had not chosen anything definite; I sat down and jotted a few scattered words and phrases onto the page, to insert into my style. But the style, just like Aunt Marcolina, stayed put. *Soeur Anne, soeur Anne* . . . Not a thing. At most, I saw the ink blacken and the paper whiten."

"But did you not eat?"

"I ate badly, fruit, manioc flour, preserves, a few roots toasted in the fire, but I would have borne everything gladly had it not been for the dreadful moral situation in which I found myself. I recited lines of poetry, speeches, passages of Latin, Gonzaga liras, Camões ottavas, décimas, a whole thirty-volume anthology. Sometimes I did exercises; at others, I would pinch my legs, but the effect was merely a physical feeling of pain or tiredness, nothing more. All silence, a vast, enormous, infinite silence, only underlined by the eternal *tick-tock* of the pendulum. *Tick-tock, tick-tock . . .*"

"Truly, enough to drive one mad."

"You will hear worse. I ought to tell you that, ever since I was left alone, I had not once looked in the mirror. My abstention had not been deliberate, there was no reason for it; it was an unconscious impulse, a fear of finding myself one person and two, in that solitary house; and if that explanation is true, nothing could be better proof of human contradiction, because after eight days, I had the notion of looking into the mirror with that very purpose, of finding myself as two. I looked, and drew back. The very glass seemed to have conspired with the rest of the universe; it did not print my shape clear and complete, but vague, smoky, diffuse, the shadow of a shadow. The reality of the laws of physics will not allow me to deny that the looking-glass did reproduce me to the letter, with the same outlines and features; it was just as it should have been. But that was not what I seemed to see. Then I truly was afraid; I attributed the phenomenon to the state of nervous excitement I was in; I was afraid of staying longer, and going mad. 'I'm leaving,' I said to myself. And I raised my arm in a gesture of bad temper, and simultaneously one of decisiveness, looking into the glass; and the gesture was there but diffuse, frayed, mutilated . . . I went inside to get dressed, murmuring to myself, coughing without a cough, shaking my clothes noisily, grumbling coldly at my buttons, just so as to be saying something. From time to time, I would steal a glance into the looking-glass; the image was the same diffusion of lines, the same decomposition of contours . . . I went on getting dressed. Suddenly, struck by some inexplicable inspiration, some unplanned impulse, I recalled . . . If you could only guess what my idea was . . ."

"Tell us."

"I was looking into the glass, with the persistence of a desperate man, contemplating my own features so blurred and incomplete, a cloud of scattered shapeless lines, when what suddenly occurred to me . . . No, you cannot guess."

"So tell us, then, tell us."

"I thought to put on my ensign's uniform. I dressed, got myself completely ready; and, when I was standing before the looking-glass, I raised my eyes, and . . . surely I need not tell you; then the glass reproduced the entire figure; not a line missing, not an outline changed; it was me myself, the ensign, who had, at last, found his external soul. The soul that had become absent with the owner of the house, scattered and fled with the slaves, there it was, gathered up in the looking-glass. Imagine a man who, emerging gradually from a lethargy, opens his eyes unable to see a thing, and then he starts to see, he differentiates people from objects, but recognises none of them individually; and then at last he does know that this one is so-and-so, and that one is what's-his-name; this here is a chair, that is a sofa. Everything returns to what it had been before his sleep. So it was with me. I was looking into the mirror, I walked this way and that, drew back, gesticulated, smiled, and the glass expressed it all. I was no longer an automaton, I was an animated being. From then on, I was a different man. Each day, at a certain time, I would dress as an ensign, and sit before the looking-glass, reading, looking, contemplating; after two, three hours, I would get undressed again. With this regime, I was able to survive another six days of solitude without feeling them . . ."

When the other men returned to their senses, the story-teller had disappeared down the stairs.

MIDNIGHT MASS

I HAVE NEVER MANAGED to understand the conversation I had with a lady, many years ago; I was seventeen, she thirty. It was Christmas Eve. Having agreed to accompany a neighbour to midnight mass, I preferred not to go to sleep; we agreed that I should wake him at midnight. The house where I was lodging was home to the notary Meneses, whose wife, for his first marriage, had been a cousin of mine. His second wife, Conceição, and her mother, had given me a warm welcome when I came from Mangaratiba to Rio de Janeiro, some months earlier, to study for my entrance examinations. I lived a calm life, in that two-storey house on Rua do Senado, with my books, few acquaintances, the occasional outing. The family was small, the notary, his wife, his mother-in-law and two slave-girls. Old customs. By ten at night, everybody was in their rooms; at ten-thirty, the house was asleep. I had never been to the theatre, and more than once, hearing

Meneses say that he was going to the theatre, I had asked him to take me along. On those occasions his mother-in-law pulled a face, and the slave-girls giggled furtively; he gave me no answer, but dressed, went out and only returned the following morning. Later I learned that the theatre was a euphemism in action. Meneses was conducting an affair with a lady who had parted from her husband, and he slept away from home once a week. At first, the existence of this concubine made Conceição suffer; but finally she resigned herself, and ended up believing it perfectly proper.

Good Conceição! They called her "the saint", and she lived up to the label, so easily did she tolerate her husband's neglect. Truly, she was moderate in temperament, never any extremes, no great weeping, no great laughter. In the episode I am referring to, she was almost like a Mohammedan; she would have accepted a harem, if it meant their saving face. May God forgive me if I misjudge her. Everything about her was attenuated and passive. Her very face was average, neither beautiful nor ugly. She was what one might call a nice person. She never spoke ill of anybody, she forgave everything. She did not know how to hate; perhaps she did not even know how to love.

On the Christmas Eve in question, the notary went to the theatre. The year was perhaps 1861 or 1862. I was already due to be back in Mangaratiba, on my holidays; but I had stayed through to Christmas "to see midnight mass in the capital". The family retired at their accustomed hour; I positioned myself in the front parlour, dressed and ready. From there I would go out to the entrance hall and leave without waking anybody. There were three keys to the front door; one had gone with the notary, I would take another, the third would stay in the house.

"Oh, but what will you do for all that time, Senhor Nogueira?" Conceição's mother had asked.

"I read, Dona Inácia."

I had a novel with me. *The Three Musketeers*, the old translation, I think from the *Jornal do Comércio*. I sat down at the table in the middle of the room, and by the light of a kerosene lamp, as the house slept, I once more mounted D'Artagnan's scrawny horse and set off on my adventures. Soon I was totally intoxicated with Dumas. The minutes flew by, hardly their custom when I am waiting for something; I heard the clocks strike eleven, barely noticing, a mere chance. However, a small noise from within roused me from my reading. It was some footsteps in the hallway that led from the drawing-room to the dining-room; I looked up; a moment later, I saw the figure of Conceição appear at the living-room door.

"You have not yet left?" she asked.

"I have not, because it is not yet midnight."

"Such patience!"

Conceição came into the living-room, shuffling her little bedroom slippers. She wore a white dressing-gown, tied loosely at her waist. Being thin, she had something of the romantic vision about her, altogether in keeping with my adventure novel. I shut the book, and she came over to sit at the chair facing mine, close to the sofa. When I asked if I had woken her, inadvertently, making some noise, she replied promptly:

"No! Not at all! I just awoke because I awoke."

I looked at her a little and doubted that claim. She did not have the eyes of somebody who had lately been sleeping; rather they looked like they had not yet fallen asleep. That observation, however, which would be worth making about another soul, I quickly dispatched, without realising that perhaps it was precisely on my account that she had not slept, and that she was lying so as not to worry or vex me. As I have already said, she was a good person, she was very good.

"But the time must be near now," I said.

"How patient of you to sit up and wait, while our neighbour sleeps! And waiting all alone! You are not afraid of souls from the other world? I believe you gave a start when you saw me."

"When I heard the footsteps I was surprised: but you appeared soon after."

"What were you reading? Don't tell me, I know, it is the novel with the Musketeers."

"Just so: it is very fine."

"You like novels?"

"I do."

"Have you read *A Moreninha*?"

"Dr Macedo's? I have it back in Mangaratiba."

"I like novels very much, but I read little, lacking the time as I do. Which novels have you read?"

I began to name a few. Conceição listened, leaning back against the headrest, her eyes peering through half-open lids, never taking them from me. From time to time she ran her tongue over her lips, to moisten them. When I finished talking, she said nothing; we remained like that a few moments. Then I saw her straighten up her head, interlacing her fingers to rest her chin on them, with her elbows on the arms of the chair, all the while keeping her big clever eyes on me.

"Perhaps she's bored," I thought.

And then, out loud:

"Dona Conceição, I believe the time is approaching, and I . . ."

"No, no, it is still early. I have only this minute consulted the clock, it is half past eleven. You have time yet. Are you, having missed the night, capable of forgoing sleep during the day?"

"I have done it before."

"I have not; missing out on a night, on the following day I am good for nothing at all, and even if it is only half an hour, I must get some sleep. But I am also getting old."

"What do you mean old, Dona Conceição!"

Such was the heat in my words that they made her smile. On the whole her movements were slow and her attitudes calm; now, however, she rose quickly, moved over to the other side of the room and took a few steps, between the window overlooking the street and the door to her husband's study. Like this, with the honest disarray that she bore about her, she made a singular impression upon me. Though thin, she had a kind of sway to her as she walked, like somebody who found it hard to carry her body; this particular manner never struck me as noticeably as it did on that night. She paused occasionally, examining a stretch of curtain or correcting the position of some object on the sideboard; finally she stopped, in front of me, with the table between us. The circle of her ideas was a narrow one; she returned to her surprise at finding me waiting up; I repeated what she already knew, that is, that I had never heard midnight mass in the capital, and I was loath to miss it.

"It is the same mass as in the country; all masses are alike."

"I believe you; but there must be more opulence here, and more people too. You know, Holy Week in the capital is much more beautiful than in the country. As for São João or Santo Antônio, I cannot say the same . . ."

Bit by bit, she had leaned forward; she had planted her elbows on the marble of the table and put her face between her open hands. Her cuffs were not buttoned up and they fell open naturally, and I saw half her arms, very light, and less thin than one might expect. The sight was not a new one to me, though neither was it a common one; at that moment, however, the impression that it made was great. Her veins were so blue that, notwithstanding the lack of light, I could count them from where I sat. Conceição's presence had served to keep me awake even more than my book. I went on saying what I thought about the feast-days in the country and in the city, and whatever else came to my mouth. I moved between subjects as I talked, not knowing why, deviating from them or returning to an earlier one, and laughing to make her smile and see her teeth that shone white, all identical. Her eyes were not quite black, but dark; her nose, which was slim and long, just slightly curved, gave her face a questioning appearance. When I raised my voice a little, she hushed me:

"Not so loud! Mother might wake."

And she remained where she was, which filled me with pleasure, so close were our faces. In truth I did not need to speak loudly to make myself heard: both of us were whispering, I more than she, for I was talking more; she, at times, would turn grave, very grave, her brow a little furrowed. Finally she tired and changed posture and position. She circled the table and came to sit beside me, on the sofa. I turned and I could see, by stealth, the tips of her slippers; but it was only for the few moments it took her to sit down, her dressing-gown was long and it quickly covered them up. I remember that they were black. Conceição said, quietly:

"Mother is a long way off, but she is a very light sleeper, if she wakes up now, poor thing, she won't be quick in getting back to sleep."

"I am just the same."

"What?" she asked, leaning in to hear me better.

I moved to sit on the chair that was right beside the sofa and repeated what I had said. She laughed at the coincidence; she slept lightly too; we were three light sleepers.

"There are moments when I am like Mother, on waking I find it hard to get back to sleep, I toss and turn in bed, this way and that, I get up, light a candle, wander about, lie down again but nothing happens."

"That is what happened to you tonight."

"No, no," she cut me short.

I could not understand her denial; perhaps she could not either. She took the ends of her dressing-gown belt and tapped her knees with them, that is, her right knee, as she had just crossed her legs. Then she recounted a story about dreams, and told me that she had only had one nightmare, as a child. She wondered whether I had them. The conversation proceeded like this, slowly, at length, without my thinking of the time or the mass. Whenever I reached the end of a story or an explanation, she would devise some other question or subject and I would resume my talking. From time to time, she would hush me:

"Not so loud, not so loud . . ."

There were also some pauses. On two other occasions, I thought I saw her drifting off to sleep; but then her eyes, closed for a moment, immediately opened with no sign of sleep or weariness, as if she had closed them to allow herself to see better. On one of those occasions, I believe she caught me absorbed in her presence and I remember that she closed them again, I could not say whether it was hurriedly or slowly. There are some impressions from that night that appear to me truncated or confused. I contradict myself, I get flustered. One of those that remain fresh in my memory is that at a given moment, she, who was merely nice, became lovely, she became very, very lovely. She was standing up, her arms crossed; I, out of respect for her, wanted to stand up, too; she would not permit it, she put a hand on my shoulder, and obliged me to remain in my seat. I supposed her to be about to speak; but she shivered, as if feeling a sudden chill, then turned away and went to sit in the chair where she had found me reading. From there she glanced back at the mirror, which hung over the sofa, and spoke of the two engravings that were on the wall.

"Those pictures are getting old. I've already asked Chiquinho to buy others."

Chiquinho was her husband. The pictures spoke of the man's principal concerns. One represented Cleopatra; I cannot recall the subject of the other, but they were women. Both rather common; I did not think them ugly at the time.

"They are lovely," I said.

"They are; but they are stained. And besides, honestly, I would prefer two images, two saints. These are better suited to a young man's bedroom or a barbershop."

"A barbershop? Surely, senhora, you have never been to the barbershop."

"But I would imagine that the patrons, while they wait, talk of girls and of courtship, and naturally the owner of the establishment likes to please their eyes with beautiful sights. For a family home, I do not think them suitable. That is what I think, but then, I think many curious things of that kind. In any case, I do not like the pictures. I have an Our Lady of Conceição, my patroness, very beautiful; but it is sculpture, not something that can be hung on the wall, nor would I want to. It is in my oratory."

The idea of the oratory transported me to the idea of the mass, reminding me that it might be late, and I wanted to say as much. I think I even opened my mouth, but then I closed it again right away when I heard what she was telling me, sweetly, gracefully, with such softness that it brought a laziness to my soul and made me forget both mass and church. She was describing her devotions as a girl and a young woman. Then she told a few stories about dances, some outings she had taken, reminiscences of her time in Paquetá, all mixed up, near uninterruptedly. When she wearied of the past, she spoke of the present, of the running of the household, the demands of family, which she had been told were many, before she was married, but which were barely anything at all. She did not tell me this, but I knew that she had married at twenty-seven.

She was no longer moving about now, as she had done before, and barely changed position. Her eyes were no longer so wide, and she began to gaze casually around the walls.

"The living-room needs repapering," she said after a little while, as if to herself.

I agreed, just to have something to say, to escape from that kind of magnetic sleepiness, or whatever it was that hindered my tongue and my senses. I wanted to end the conversation, and also I did not; I made an effort to pull away from her eyes, and I did pull away from them out of a feeling of respect; but the idea that it might look like boredom, when it was not, brought my eyes back to Conceição. The conversation was dying away. On the street, total silence.

Finally we remained, for a while – I cannot say for how long – absolutely quiet. The only slight noise was a mouse nibbling away in the study, which woke me from that sort of drowsiness; I wanted to say something about it, but I could not find the way. Conceição appeared to be daydreaming. Suddenly I heard a knock on the window, from outside, and a voice calling out: "Midnight mass! Midnight mass!"

"There is your companion," she said, getting up. "How funny; it was you who was to have woken him, and he has come to wake you. Go, then – it must be time; farewell."

"It is time already?" I asked.

"Of course."

"Midnight mass!" the voice repeated from outside, knocking.

"Go, go, do not make them wait. The fault is mine. Adieu; until tomorrow."

And with that same swaying of her body, Conceição slipped away down the hallway, treading softly. I went outside and found our neighbour waiting. We walked from there to the church. During the mass, the figure of Conceição appeared more than once, between me and the priest; put that down to my seventeen years. The following morning, at breakfast, I talked about the midnight mass and the people who were at the church without arousing any particular curiosity from Conceição. During the day, I found her just as ever, natural, kind, with nothing to remind me of the previous night's conversation. Around New Year I travelled

MACHADO DE ASSIS

MACHADO DE ASSIS, who came to be the finest prose-writer in the Portuguese language, died on September 29th last, in Rio de Janeiro, the city where he was born in 1839, and which he never left. He divided his time between the Ministry of Industry, where he was a section head, his presidency of the Brazilian Academy, and his literary activity, which was exemplary.

A poet, a novelist and sometimes also an author of criticism and theatre, he was a rare and perfect writer. Coming out of our romantic movement, he soon abandoned it to resume the classical tradition, though one that was personal and always free. His is a unique case, and he seems a sort of marvel, in a milieu where the influence of romanticism remains strong. Machado de Assis was sober. He was subtle and wise. A superior ironist, an assured psychologist, he liked to involve himself in paradoxes and fantasies. He might remind you of Lucian and of Anatole France. But his style is his own, for the originality of his thinking.

In the 17th century, they would have called him a moralist. He was often a Swift, but without anger, a Swift full of finesse, gently disillusioned.

He was of the same breed as the greatest writers, for his elegant and elastic power, for that simplicity that was ultimately so complex just as things of genius are, the way water is produced by things in nature. Nobody handled the adjective better than he.

A master of language, he was also a master of the Portuguese tongue in particular, one of those who knew it best. And we are not speaking here of a mere richness of vocabulary, which is not uncommon and is fundamentally a matter of memory, but of an identification, as if subterranean, with the psychological sources of expression, which can only come from true culture.

His art is bitter. It is the serenity of the thinker consoling himself for life. A sceptic, his scepticism still did not make him turn towards it. He was perhaps lacking in rather more positive joy, more physical health, to have the simple sensuality of living, the animality that sings in the artist. And his poems and novels suffer from this. But so many of his stories are and remain models. His letters are masterpieces of charm, of moderation, of discreet goodness. He wrote sonnets worthy of Camões.

The man in him was delightful, a little shy, even naïve on many matters, which his moral delicacy would not allow his criticism to touch. Likewise in his academic and official duties, which he always fulfilled with honest zeal and sincere faith. A director of accounting at the Ministry, this disheartened sceptic did believe in accounting.

Inalterably courteous, with no sourness or posturing, taking care of art, he did not concern himself with attacks or arguments. His polished dignity would have found no use for such things. He lived in tranquillity for Letters, surrounded by the affection or respect of intelligent men, the admirable dedication of his wife, and beautiful female friendships. He leaves us with the memory of a delightful spirit and an exquisitely delicate heart.

Tristão da Cunha, 1908

TRANSLATOR'S NOTE

I've read various Machado de Assis translations, in bits and pieces, over the years. There are many I like, each of them doing something quite different. This particular translation leans deliberately towards an older voice – there's some starch in his sentences, and a bit of height to his diction, which I feel suits him. I think keeping a reader constantly aware that this is a man writing 140 years ago – albeit quite idiosyncratically – is useful for sharpening those ways in which he does actually feel surprisingly modern.

Putting on a 19th-century voice isn't always the easiest solution for a translator, however, and it risks a drift into apparent parody, which I hope the voice in this collection avoids. Needless to say, if it does work, I need to acknowledge the fine tuning and impeccable instincts of Rory Williamson and Robina Pelham Burn, who respectively edited and copy-edited the text. Both were tactful and light-handed, but every small change they contributed made things better. (It goes without saying, if this voice does not work, the fault is mine.)

I began my translation in Iowa City, as translator in residence at the university there, and I must thank my friend Aron Aji, who gave me that special opportunity, along with the rest of the University of Iowa staff, for the warm welcome. I shared the earliest drafts of "The Alienist" with a group of brilliant MFA students; this was intended mainly to show them just how bad my drafts were, but I also ended up benefiting from their ideas. One neat little bit of wordplay in particular belongs to Muhua Yang; and Davide Vigliotti has got a helpful word in there, too. While I'm remembering Iowa, I should also thank Robin and Kim at the Historic Phillips House, who for six weeks gave me a very lovely home in theirs. I do hope to go back.

My work on this book coincided with the establishing of PELTA, the Portuguese-English Literary Translators Association, and I have taken advantage of many colleagues from that gang, too. Among them, Elton Uliana, who answered some last-minute questions; my fellow Machado de Assis story translator Margaret Jull Costa, who generously lent me her favourite; and the most grateful thanks, of course, to the committee who made PELTA happen.

Finally, I should acknowledge some eleventh-hour assistance from my mother while I was translating the afterword. The piece in question is a brief personal appreciation of Machado de Assis, written on the occasion of his death, by Tristão da Cunha, who knew him. Tristão was himself a writer and translator, and also, as it happens, the great-grandfather of this one.

D.H.

STEFAN ZWEIG · EDGAR ALLAN POE · ISAAC BABEL
TOMÁS GONZÁLEZ · ULRICH PLENZDORF · JOSEPH KESSEL
VELIBOR ČOLIĆ · LOUISE DE VILMORIN · MARCEL AYMÉ
ALEXANDER PUSHKIN · MAXIM BILLER · JULIEN GRACQ
BROTHERS GRIMM · HUGO VON HOFMANNSTHAL
GEORGE SAND · PHILIPPE BEAUSSANT · IVÁN REPILA
E.T.A. HOFFMANN · ALEXANDER LERNET-HOLENIA
YASUSHI INOUE · HENRY JAMES · FRIEDRICH TORBERG
ARTHUR SCHNITZLER · ANTOINE DE SAINT-EXUPÉRY
MACHI TAWARA · GAITO GAZDANOV · HERMANN HESSE
LOUIS COUPERUS · JAN JACOB SLAUERHOFF
PAUL MORAND · MARK TWAIN · PAUL FOURNEL
ANTAL SZERB · JONA OBERSKI · MEDARDO FRAILE
HÉCTOR ABAD · PETER HANDKE · ERNST WEISS
PENELOPE DELTA · RAYMOND RADIGUET · PETR KRÁL
ITALO SVEVO · RÉGIS DEBRAY · BRUNO SCHULZ · TEFFI
EGON HOSTOVSKÝ · JOHANNES URZIDIL · JÓZEF WITTLIN